Opportunities

of a

Lifetime

Robert Shafer

ISBN 978-1-0980-2327-0 (paperback)
ISBN 978-1-0980-2328-7 (digital)

Christian Faith Publishing, Inc.
832 Park Avenue
Meadville, PA 16335
www.christianfaithpublishing.com

Printed in the United States of America

To Joyce, who I'm sure has entered the gates of heaven and is right now in a better life waiting for me. Her passing I am sure is the best solution for her to help me cope with the stress I feel. I know that she will continue to bless all of us with her love and special adorations for us that only she could place in God's grace.

Joyce was an avid enabler who inspired me to continue writing my stories, as an author, and each story will have an inspirational ending to credit her. Joyce was well liked by everyone and had been active in New Hackensack Church for over fifty years. I am sure our Creator knows how well. Many of our friends there have many memories of her.

The ASPCA in Hyde Park were always ready to adopt any animal for her. Joyce was very active there. She often reminded all of the people and friends at the shelter in Hyde Park, "Just remember I want an old small fluffy white dog." We still have one who misses her greatly.

CONTENTS

PREFACE

The stories in this book follow a "young boy growing up in the country." It covers my life story, filled with many challenges, starting from age three to the ripe old age of twenty-five, although there are some overlaps in the chapters that describe the many facets of boyhood.

I'm contemplating on writing a follow-up story detailing the last half of my life until my present age of seventy-eight. I would like to offer my thanks to my wife Joyce for her patience in reviewing my writings during the last six months. Rewrites were much easier to make if there was any conflict.

Thank you. I hope that you will be interested.

CHAPTER 1

Early Memories: Living with My Grandparents

The earliest memories I can recall includes Mom, Dad, and myself and the period when we first moved into an apartment in my grandfather and grandmother's home.

My father met my mother in the late 1930s. I believe he met her when they went to a hoedown (a farm dance party). Dad was a caller for square dances and apparently was quite good at it. They got married in the Polish Church in Adams and soon I appeared! Dad and Mom needed a place to live. They moved into my grandparents' home on Crotteau Street in Adams, Massachusetts. My other siblings, Mary, Ed, Pat, and John, were not yet in the picture and will show up later on.

I do not know how to spell my grandparents' Polish names, so I used Google's Cortana. The Polish names are "Jah-Goo" for Grandpa and "Gigi" for Grandma. For simplicity, I will continue using their English equivalent.

My grandparents occupied the first-floor apartment, along with my uncle Henry and my aunt Alice, who lived in the larger first-floor apartment. We were in the smaller second-floor apartment. The house was built with a first-floor porch and another second-floor porch on both the front and back sides of the building. The porches were painted gray, and the rest of the house was painted yellow. The porches were great for watching activities at the street level. The Massachusetts National Guard was stationed just a short distance up the street, and the guardsmen marched by in local events. They eventually went off to war in the Pacific against Japan. Behind the house was a two-car garage with pigeonholes at the top of the doorways. There was a chicken coop and a small garden with pear, plum, and crabapple trees in the yard.

The year was 1943 and the world was at war with Germany, Italy, and Japan. There was a huge RCA console in Grandpa's living room. The family listened to President Roosevelt's "Day of Infamy" speech on it in 1941. Dad and I listened to the war stories. We all listened to the Polish music. Grandpa and Grandma spoke very little English, but there were a lot of local Polish people who lived in that part of town, so radios paid them tribute. The town actually was split almost exactly in half between the French side and the Polish side.

Dad worked at the local limestone business in Adams. He needed a car badly. Finally, he found one that needed to be repaired, an old Model A Ford automobile whose engine was pretty well shot. I know he didn't have a lot of money to spend, but he intended to repair it.

Dad proved to be a very gifted mechanic. He was able to rebuild an engine with amazing dexterity. Being so mechanically astute, Dad made a good purchase when he found a really old Ford automobile and it sure needed work. I remember him starting the car by turning a hand crank. The crank had to be inserted into the bumper. There was about 25,000 miles on the odometer. I remember watching Dad struggle to start the engine. It was difficult and would only start when cranked by hand with the starter crank. When the engine started, it belched plenty of smoke and it was obvious that the repairs were necessary right away. He would have to stop the engine and start the engine repairs as soon as he acquired the tools and parts.

The engine needed new spark plugs and ring and a valve replacement. These repairs would make it start easier and stop the engine from burning oil. Due to the metallurgy of the times, it was normal to have excessive wear of these parts when there was such low mileage.

Dad tackled the repair to save money (of which we had little). I was three years old at the time and watched with unabashed curiosity. Dad took the time to show me what the parts were and how he was going to accomplish the repair. I admit that I only had a vague idea of what he was talking about. With plenty of onlookers, both friends and neighbors, Dad took the engine apart in the backyard. He used his own tools and asked if anyone else had the additional tools he still needed. He had good support.

Grandpa and others borrowed tools from friends. Fascinated by all of this, I watched him completely rebuild the engine. First he removed any parts that were attached to the engine necessary to obtain access to the engine block containing the valves and rings. After removing and cleaning the engine block, cylinders, etc., he used a special sleeve designed to allow the cylinders to be reinstalled with the new rings and slid the cylinders and the replaced rings into the cylinder ports of the engine. The block was cleaned and ground to tolerance by a local shop. Dad replaced the valves and reinstalled the engine as it was but with new parts and seals. He then replaced the carburetor, cables, and hoses. Then he declared, "There, it is done."

Dad showed me how to use the starter crank without getting my arm or nose broken if the crank kicked back a little. I helped to start the car by twisting the starter crank, while he fiddled with the spark and gas levers. It started on the second turn with just a small puff of smoke that gradually cleared. I was proud of being able to help.

Uncle Henry and Aunt Alice would visit often, and I remember during one visit, my dad asked me to go upstairs and get two beers. I trudged up the sixteen-stair steps to our apartment. The stairs were like a mountain to me, and I was determined to complete my mission. I grabbed two bottles from the icebox.

Uncle Henry had asked for ale (which came in a green bottle), and the other was beer (in a brown bottle) for Dad. As I started down the stairs, my feet slid out from under me, and I proceeded to go down the stairs in a rather unorthodox way, rolling and bouncing all the way down. I arrived with a jolt but managed to save both bottles and my neck. When Mom arrived breathless at the bottom of the stairs, she was yelling at Dad, "Next time get your own beer! Are you okay, Bobby?"

I smiled at her and showed Mom my prizes saying, "See, they're not even broken."

It was about this time that we heard the music on Crotteau Street. We rushed to the windows and then to the porch, watching an army unit going by. Behind the army color guard was a band playing a marching tune. It was followed by a company of soldiers from the armory. Every soldier carried a rifle on his shoulder. They looked sharp in their uniforms as they marched toward war. Shortly after this, we moved to another apartment.

CHAPTER 2

Need for a Larger Apartment

O ur family had gotten bigger with the arrival of Mary and Ed. Mom and Dad found a downstairs apartment in a four-family apartment building on Miller Street in Adams, and we moved there early in 1944. It was a spacious apartment with two bedrooms, living room, and a large kitchen. It had a shared back porch for the two ground-floor apartments and also another similar porch upstairs for the upstairs apartments. There was only one problem with the building—cockroaches. They were everywhere and very hardy. It was almost impossible to get rid of them. One apartment would use a cockroach bomb (a pressurized metal cylinder filled with pesticide), but the cockroaches would just move on to one or more of the other apartments. One of the cockroaches' favorite hiding spaces was in the stove. Mary and I took it upon ourselves to kill as many of these bugs as we could. Daily we would take the gas knobs off the stove and light a match to kill them. This killed whatever bug happened to be hiding in there at the time, but because they were throughout the building, we would have to have the whole building exterminated to get rid of them.

Life at the apartment building was full of new things for us. We now had more friends to play with and new things to do.

Monthly during the summer, one of our neighbors would provide the neighborhood entertainment by setting up a 16 mm sound movie camera, mounting it on a tripod on the porch, renting films from the library, and setting up a screen made from a large white sheet in front of the garbage area. All the neighborhood kids were invited. An average of twenty kids and some adults participated. The show started after dusk complete with *Looney Tunes* and Warner Brothers news clippings from the war effort. We had cartoons like Bugs Bunny, Road Runner, Porky Pig, and any others that were available. Everyone made popcorn, and the show lasted about an hour. To wash down the popcorn, we had large bottles of soda from the Squeeze Bottling Company. At that time, soda sold for five cents a bottle and fifteen cents a quart. The Squeeze Bottling Company had a five-cent return on their bottles as they used them over and over again. Coke was another favorite in the old-fashioned bottle with the company location pressed into the bottom of the bottle. It was always amazing to see how far away some of those locations were. There were no canned drinks at that time as the pop-top had yet to be invented.

That winter, we did our first ice-skating. Ice-skating was very popular in the area. It was much colder then, and when it did get cold, it lasted. The town recreation department made a rectangular dam on the local ball field and flooded a rink area of about seventy-five feet by two hundred feet. They used a fire hose and obtained the water from a nearby fireplug. A caretaker for the train crossing volunteered to ensure that the ice was in great shape all the time. His real job was to man the road crossing with a stop sign in his hand to control traffic for the one or two trains a day that used the tracks running through our area. The attendant recruited a few good helpers like me. What kid wouldn't enjoy spraying the ice with a large fire hose? A daily light spraying on the surface of the ice kept the ice hard and looking like glass, providing a really nice finish to skate on.

Dad now had a trucking business. He delivered limestone to the record companies, and he always brought home 78 rpm and 45 rpm phonograph records. The limestone that Dad delivered was used in the manufacturing process of these records. All the records had one song on each side, since long-playing 33 rpm albums had not yet come to market. We had a huge collection. Some of the songs were okay, but most were rejects. Two that I remember were "Mean to Me" and another "Humphrey, the Sweet Singing Pig," and others were Roy Rogers and Gene Autry songs or swing and sway music popular in the late 1930s and early 1940 era. The sound quality was less than desirable because most of these records came off the reject pile. The needles on the record player were about the size of a one-inch nail. The composition of the material was softer than the more modem vinyl records of today. The point of the needle was rather blunt and tended to wear the records out very fast. The records also scratched rather easily.

That year, I started school in an all-day preprimary class in our local elementary school. That was also the year that President Roosevelt died. Not really understanding the importance of this event, we listened in class to the announcement over the school speaker system. Everyone held a moment of silence and then did the Pledge of Allegiance in a solemn moment of grief. Someone named Harry Truman took over.

Dad was drafted by Uncle Sam in early 1945 and went off to war with the Navy Seabees. He shipped out to the Solomon Islands in the South Pacific where he helped build airfields and other facilities. That was where he learned the skills of a bulldozer operator, which served him well in his future endeavors. The day Dad left for the service, practically the whole neighborhood of kids gathered at the railroad tracks at the end of our road. Everyone was sure that my father was on the first train that we saw go by and heading out to war. We waved until it was well past. Well, we thought that was the way it was anyway, but to tell the truth, we weren't too knowledgeable of train schedules and destinations.

While Dad was away, extra chores came my way. Keeping the fires going became part of my daily routine, and I remember bringing the heavy coal bucket filled with coal from our coal bin up the cellar stairs. That was quite a load for a five-year-old. Our coal bin was a source of entertainment when the coal was delivered by the coal company truck. It was always a big show to watch the coal come down the chute and build a substantial pile in the basement coal bin.

We had a lot of snow during that time, and shoveling the steps and walkways was another task that I inherited. Every kid in the apartments shared shoveling the driveway. The kids had fun shoveling the snow in the front of every house. Every house had snow igloos and snow forts and had a supply of snowballs for the inevitable snowball fights.

Life was rather simple at the time. The milkman delivered milk in quart bottles made of glass. The cream would separate and actually pop the bottle's cover, sometimes lifting the cover as high as two inches. It was always a treat to take the cream off the top of the milk and using the butter churner whip the cream for strawberry shortcake. I would pick strawberries from the nearby fields and Mom would make the biscuits.

We had an icebox for household items needing refrigeration. The iceman delivered blocks of ice every week using a horse-drawn wagon. The huge blocks of ice on his wagon were kept cold by being covered with straw. He used large steel hooks to maneuver the large blocks to a work area on the wagon and then used an icepick to chip the ice into manageably sized blocks. Using large tongs, he carried the blocks into the house and loaded the icebox.

The town used a road grader to plow our road in the winter, its large low-slung blades serving as snowplows. In the spring, they used a mixture of small stones covered with oil to surface our road and packed it down with a steamroller. Belching huge clouds of steam, the huge monster was a sight to behold.

Behind the apartments was a garbage pit where we burned most refuse. A pail was used to save meal remnants and other edible garbage for the town farm of Adams. It was known as slop. Weekly, an employee of the farm was sent to collect it and the farm used it as food for the pigs.

The apartments had coal stoves for heating and synthetic gas for cooking. The gas was manufactured from coal by Berkshire Gas in Pittsfield, Massachusetts, and delivered through a distribution system to homes in the more densely populated areas. Hot water for bathing, dishwashing, and other hot water needs was heated in kettles on the gas burners.

It was a time of rationing, and Mom doled out her monthly ration coupons wisely for gasoline, sugar, and the like. We were all encouraged to save Liberty stamps as a fund-raiser for the government's efforts to pay for the war. They were five cents each and sold through the US Post Office. They were considered a form of savings and placed in small booklets by the purchaser to be cashed in after the war.

Butter was used only for the war effort and was stored in huge government storehouses. Oleomargarine was manufactured as a substitute for butter. Everyone wanted to be the one to squeeze the cellophane package with its yellow dot in the center to get the butter-color spread throughout. It didn't taste much like butter, probably a taste closer to lard than anything, but it served its purpose.

To help ends meet, Mom worked at the Sprague Electric Company plant in North Adams as a solderer. Sprague's main product was electric capacitors. With Mom working, we spent quite a bit of time with our aunt who was our babysitter. The money Mom made was necessary to keep us fed and clothed. Dad sent money, but the service pay was rather weak those days. Mom ran a tab at George's Supermarket. George, the owner, was a generous man, keeping a running tab that was always quite high. Every week, Mom dutifully paid what she could.

The phonograph records that Dad had brought home before he left for the service were by this time of such poor quality that I brought most of them to the school for school projects. The records were softened in hot water and formed into candy dishes and ashtrays. The kids in the class used them as presents to their families. They were great projects and made useful gifts.

Early in 1946, Dad came home from the navy. Two more children, Pat and John, quickly appeared and space became a premium.

We finally got all the neighbors to use insecticide bombs for cockroaches at the same time. Everyone evacuated the building until the gas subsided. This killed off most of the roaches and they were never a problem after that.

On holidays, we would have a picnic at the state park in Savoy. The river running through the park was dammed by the state, and a small swimming area was available that was considered safe for young kids. A bridge crossed the dam from the parking lot. The shade of the evergreen trees made a comfortable surrounding where picnic tables, rock fireplaces with grills, and potable water were available. The picnics were fun with the main activity centering on hamburgers, hot dogs, toasted marshmallows, and baseball. There were small tributary streams where we attempted to catch small trout and frogs that were common in the freshwater.

Mom had a washing machine with a wringer mechanism on the top. We liked to play with the rollers while they turned. This turned out to be a near disaster for my brother Ed when he copied Mary and me. Suddenly, the rollers grabbed his hand, and within moments, his arm was in the wringer. The wringer jammed and we were in a panic to get him free. Mom had Ed's arm checked by the doctor, and except for a little scarring, he suffered no great harm. Ed always seemed to need more doctoring than the rest of us. I remember the doctor removing his tonsils on the kitchen table. I think he was the only one in the family who needed that operation.

As the children got bigger, it was obvious that we needed more room. Wanting their own home, Dad and Mom went house hunting. In 1947, we moved to the farm.

Pictured above is the farm thirty years after we first moved in. The house had been resided with aluminum siding. The car, a 1988 Olds, is mine. Structural changes in the house include removal of the mudroom and addition of a picture window thereby enlarging the living room. Other than that, the house and grounds still have the original appearance.

CHAPTER 3

Moving to the Farm

After passing one house on the left side of the road, one house on the right side of the road, and then a farmhouse with a long steep driveway (Sturtevant's) on the right, suddenly I saw it! The house on the next parcel of land, next door to Sturtevant's, was white with a barn in the backyard and a small creek running in front of the house. The driveway had a bridge that went all the way to a red barn. I just knew that this was the place! Everything matched just as Mom had described it. I couldn't wait to tell everyone that I had seen it. I was so excited. It was just as I had pictured it and I had found it!

Not daring to go onto the property, because after all we did not yet own it, I turned around and headed for home. It was downhill most of the way. Arriving, I quickly dismounted from my bicycle and shouted, "Mom! I saw our house!"

She laughed and said, "Well, now all we have to do is to get the bank to loan us the money." After the mortgage was approved, we started on upgrading the farmhouse.

Dwellings on the property included the house, barn, chicken coup, workshop, and outhouse bathroom.

Our new home had three bedrooms, a small kitchen, a narrow bathroom, and a large living room that was the full width of the house. The living room had a large-sized window that gave light to the living room and provided a beautiful view of the mountains. There was a mudroom at the back of the house with an entrance from outside and access to the basement. There were also two stoves, one in the kitchen with propane gas for the burners and wood for heat and another free-standing stove in the living room that used kerosene as fuel. All in all, they kept the inside temperature in check. I was responsible of refilling the kerosene container, when the kerosene was low, and supply the kitchen with wood. The propane was supplied with a local vendor.

The original structure of the house was a large chicken coop. Our new house might have been described as a farmhouse, but a cottage might have been more appropriate. Opening the inside door from the back of the house was a mudroom entrance where there was a wooden ladder that gave access to the attic and another ladder down to a dirt floor basement. Both entrances had very little room to maneuver in. Inside the dirt floor basement was a small room that measured five feet high and had a width of twenty-four feet.

The balance of the downstairs was designed as a support for the upstairs living room and bedroom, with one closet on the top floor. It had clearance of three feet for the rest of the building.

That basement room housed a covered well, a pump, and piping for the kitchen and the bathroom. A small trickle of water flowed toward the septic field at the east side of the house. Our source of water was the well, which was about fifteen feet in depth. On the average, the well water's depth was about five feet. There was an electric pump, with appropriate pressure switches, and a storage tank for our daily water usage and it was connected to the piping. I do recall seeing the well actually filled to the brim, when the snow cover melted in the spring.

A secondary source of water was from the stream and the dam outside of the house. This water was connected only to the bathroom, since at times the water did not meet sanitary conditions because the high water in the dam comes from the high runoff of snowmelt from the fields, above our property.

On the other hand, during the summer when there's low water, we added twelve inches of concrete to the walls of the dam for extra water. Even with the dam being taller, with heavy rainstorms came mud. We had to open up the dam every year to clean mud from the fields collected in the dam's backwater. The cultured fields, just south of our property, were mostly cornfields, and the annual snowmelt allowed the muddy drainage to completely fill the dam with mud and also strain the downstream openings of our bridge. At times, the large flow of water threatened the structure of the dam and bridge openings. So we had to fill the openings below the dam and bridge with large boulders and timbers to ensure the bridge's integrity and open the water flow control openings inside the dam to lower the pressure. On occasion, the town helped us by supplying water from a fire engine's tank and using their high-pressure hoses to clean the mud from the pond behind the dam.

Neither of the water supplies were 100 percent dependable. During dry spells, we used milk cans to capture drinkable water that flowed from a six-inch water pipe near the bottom of the hill at Fisk Road. The water came from a natural source out from a low-lying area near our home on Miller Street. Many chose to use this water since it's drinkable. This source was eventually closed by the board of health.

At times, when the water sources were low, Dad would use the corner edge of the rooftop to shower and he would encourage us to use it. Because it was easily viewed by automobiles on West Road, we used our bathing suits. We also had a two-seater outhouse that got a lot of use! The long-range plan was drilling for an artesian well.

There were many chores to be accomplished in our continued activities at the farm. From spring and into the fall, we used a push lawn mower to mow our lawns. The leaves needed to be raked in the fall and crushed with the lawn mower. We used the shredded leaves to keep the pens clean for our animals. There was plenty of snow in the winter, and we spent plenty of effort and time shoveling it.

Our everyday chores included taking care of the many different animals in the barn. These chores were shared with my brother Ed and much later with my other brother John. We purchased a heifer cow for our milk, two dozen chicks for eventual eggs, rabbits for stew, and two piglets that Grandpa would eventually butcher.

As a boy, Dad lived on a dairy farm in Cheshire, Massachusetts. He knew the heifer needed to be two to three years old and would have to be impregnated by that time. The heifer then carried the calf for eight to nine months. The calf was expected to be born about this time. The heifer then would be called a cow. Immediately, the newly arrived calf would feed on the cow's utters (four to choose from). Milk production would begin about seven to nine weeks after the calf was born. Then the real work for us was next.

We trapped pigeons in my grandpa and grandma's backyard. Using a large cardboard box and propping it up with a stick, we attached a long string to the stick, and when a pigeon entered the box area, we pulled the string, catching the pigeon as it ate the chicken feed bait.

After we captured a couple of pigeons, we would use another box to bring them to the farm. They were released at the farm and spent most of their time on the roof of the barn or on the family clothesline. During inclement weather, they would enter the barn using the hayloft entrance on the front of the barn. After a while, we attracted more pigeons and they multiplied on their own. Some pigeons were used at times for a squab dinner.

While waiting for the calf to arrive, we had a lot of work to do. We had to fence the backyard, using posts and barbed wire, and fix the stations and floors inside the barn, where the cows would be held. We put more hay, from Sturtevant's farm next door, in the upstairs loft of the barn. (We spent a lot of time helping them fill their own barn!) We purchased milk pails for milking and milk cans for storage of water. We also shored up our barn's structure and painted the barn's exterior. It seemed that the continued work would take forever!

Dad purchased a couple of truckloads of peastone gravel to repair the puddled areas and frost heaves of the driveway. Dad, Ed, and I were construction engineers on the job! The driveway really needed the smoothing effect. Our driveway was quite long. From the road, it crossed the bridge over the stream on the front side of our lot and then to the barn and measured approximately 120 feet long. It widened in the middle with a twenty-foot parking spot near the house and a twenty-foot turnaround that formed a "Y" in the middle section. Altogether, it was a considerable task!

Dad arranged for pasture rights for our cow Susie, from the Micklejohn family, about a mile south and down the road to the pasture area. It was not dangerous because the vehicular traffic was very low.

When we first moved to the farm, the West Road was a very narrow dirt road with very little car traffic. Today the road is a wide and busy blacktop two-lane highway.

It took nine months for our cow to have her calf. Every family member was fascinated with the birth of her cow. After the calf was born, the calf fed on the mother's teats for ten to twelve weeks and then we had to start milking the cow. Ed and I shared the effort and we had competition between us. Ed was more efficient and he finally showed me his expertise!

CHAPTER 4

How I First Learned to Repair Televisions

W hen I entered the US Air Force from my hometown, I had no knowledge whatsoever of any electronics, especially the new technologies, and I needed to repair the newest electronic devices, called television.

I knew that there were companies like GE, RCA Victor, and others developing TV as we knew it then. During the 1939 World's Fair, the introduction this new technology was televised using a five-inch screen. They were received at the fair, having been transmitted from Albany, New York, by RCA Victor. When television became popular, shows like *Howdy Doody*, *Dick Clark's American Bandstand*, *the Ed Sullivan Show*, *What's Behind the Green Door*, and others were created from old radio shows. In the past, we listened to our radio to hear all these shows. That would change.

When we first moved to the West Road where we lived, our neighbors had purchased an RCA television with a five-inch display. They also purchased a large magnifying glass that they attached to their TV. This caused the scan lines to have more space between them. It did make their TV into a larger twelve-inch viewing screen. The video quality was not as good as the five-inch cathode-ray tube in their RCA set, but it was easier for any friends who were invited to visit. Everyone was glad they had bought the TV, especially with the larger viewing screen with the magnifier attachment. They enjoyed buttered popcorn and apple cider when they arrived.

Because of poor signals in the Berkshire Valley, an electric repeater station had been installed on top of the mountain with a thirty-five-foot antenna tower with bright shiny red signal lights attached to warn approaching aircraft about Mount Greylock. At 3, 410 feet tall, Mount Greylock had a fifty-foot-plus granite memorial tower, with a large glass dome that was five-foot in circumference, and it had powerful rotating white lights. The antenna was the second tower that extended far above the mountaintop (the first one was the memorial tower), and the two towers caused a lot of local residents to worry about the possibilities of a plane crashing into one of them. In fact, there is a small dedicated display close to the top of the mountain in memory of a recent plane crash.

Both towers were eventually taken down because of an edict from the state of Massachusetts. The memorial tower was rebuilt in about two years, and this was a result of a powerful fight between the Massachusetts politicians from Boston and the Adams town officials.

A great majority of Adams residents expressed strong support for the rebuilding of the memorial tower. Adams won!

The granite took a long time to replace. Improvements during the rebuilding of the monument included placement of the granite with better sealing, reduced lighting from the tower, better facilities with parking lots, other trails to the picnic areas, and more restaurants. The power lines from Adams were improved. Some people would think that the politicians might be gloating about their successful turnaround, but the people of Adams were still impressed with the outcome of the fight.

It took several years to totally rebuild the monument. I cannot tell you what was done with the repeater, but the signal had been replaced with new and more powerful television stations from Albany and other surrounding cities by the time I returned from the US Air Force after four years of service.

We eventually purchased a Westinghouse TV that had a seventeen-inch black-and-white monitor for our home. We received two UHF channels on it, both from the repeater. Occasionally, the weather permitted a third channel, from a signal coming from an antenna south of us. The signal originated from a television station near the Pittsfield area. This required a rotor, a control box, and wiring that allowed the antenna to swing in a southerly direction. It also was a UHF channel.

The antenna necessary to transmit the UHF from the mountaintop was approximately the same height as the monument built to honor the Massachusetts veterans. Our signal at home was so strong that it required adding resistors in series with the antenna wires so as not to overload the set. With that changed, we could view the pictures broadcast from the repeater transmitter at Mount Greylock.

Reviving an old tradition, we decided to make popcorn and apple cider for our guests, which was exactly what the neighbors had done for their visitors in the past. Their farm had a lot of apples on their apple trees and were going to waste, and they said we could use all we wanted!

The apples for our first cider came from those trees, but the cider was made with a cider press at another of our neighboring farm.

Eventually I worked at that farm and operated the cider press, which, when operated, poured thirty gallons of apple juice for our barrel. We used gallon bottles to carry the cider to our home. The mash was placed in bushel baskets and fed to our pigs. Since the barrel were significantly heavy, this caused problems in lowering the barrel down the narrow basement steps. Using the basement was necessary to store the cider in a cool place. We laid the barrel horizontally on the right wall of our basement onto wooden planks and then removed the cork stopper to pour the ingredients into the barrel that were necessary to develop the cider. My grandfather helped us by giving us the proper proportions of the ingredients. Those ingredients, besides the apple juice from the jugs, were generally raisins, vinegar, and granulated sugar. The cider would ferment into sweet apple cider, then next into hard cider, and eventually with additional fermentation a very strong apple liquor. Sampling it proved that Grandpa knew his stuff!

Installing the antennas and cabling were my first efforts in understanding television. The next efforts were accomplished during my four years of education and job responsibilities in electronics in the US Air Force. I continued those efforts, which are detailed in the succeeding chapters, to maintain the family's necessary income level and retain our lifestyle.

CHAPTER 5

Exploring Cole Mountain: Gold Fever!

During the summer of 1949, a couple of my friends and I decided to explore Cole Mountain. Local farmers claimed that in the past, gold mining operations took place on the mountain during the 1920s and 1930s. Comparatively, Cole Mountain is a small ridge nearly ten miles long and approximately 1,500 feet in height attached to a major ridge called Mount Greylock with a comparative height of 3,420 feet, the tallest mountain in Massachusetts.

We had taken many hikes over the years climbing to the top of Mount Greylock, but those adventures never involved gold mining that anyone knew of. We definitely had gold fever!

Cole Mountain was just south and west of West Road in Adams, Massachusetts, and then north to south toward Cheshire, Massachusetts.

Just off West Road, there are many ponds and small streams that flow in an easterly direction to a reservoir on Reservoir Road. It is one of the major sources of drinkable water for the town of Adams. This source is augmented with artesian wells drilled deep in the nearby grounds.

My father had a skill called water witching, and he was very popular with the locals (he used forked apple tree limbs to find the deep water in artesian wells). He located many wells that were drilled successfully and was blessed with small donations for his task. The *North Adams Transcript*, a local newspaper, printed his story and he was the toast of the town.

The ponds and streams off West Road support fish, frogs, pollywogs, snakes, birds, and other animals. Many of these birds, crows, hawks, and mankind prove deadly toward these populations. My father loved for us to harvest the green leaper frogs so that he could have the legs for dinner.

We started searching on the top of the north end of the ridge and followed deer trails that seemed to have some activity and direction that might be of interest. Finding very little to indicate structures or cavelike openings, we started down the side of the mountain. Then we started seeing a lot of fox and raccoon dens, but we didn't have much success in general. We didn't find any caves so all three of us separated and continued to search along the middle of the mountainside looking for appropriate openings that might show some promise.

Lo and behold, we discovered an opening near a rock aperture that appeared to be interesting. It was large enough to interest us. We gathered together around the opening, which was approximately a twenty-four to thirty inches in diameter. It seemed to be just larger than our chests. As we approached it, we took our flashlights and looked downward into the hole. It seemed to go down about eight feet and into a large room of about 10 x 15 feet in area. Both Dick and Ed had larger chests than me, and they felt comfortable that they could fit through the hole, so I being of smaller build could also. It was an exciting discovery! With our flashlights, we decided to try to go down into the cavelike room. This eventually proved to be true as we were successful in entering the room. We scanned the room with our lights and perused every inch.

Viola! This just might be our gold mine!

It was a little claustrophobic in the cave, so we were afraid to stay too long. We found an old lantern on the floor, but it literally fell apart when we lifted the handle. The glass was broken and the base unit separated when we picked it up. Nevertheless, it was exciting. We immediately envisioned a miner using this lantern in his search for gold in the cave. The flashlight batteries were getting low, so we progressed back to the opening and climbed out exhausted, vowing to return another day to follow up our discovery. Although I did return, as a group, we never did return to the cave.

We had many other interesting activities yet to discover. I will briefly tell you about them and then tell you about my next climb going to the cave.

Fishing was a new sport to us. We fished the Hoosic River in Adams and Cheshire, the Green River in Williamstown, Dean's brook, Cheshire Lake, and other locations. Hunting was also new. Over the years, we spent a lot of time hunting deer and rabbits around our area forests. Later we expanded our hunting into Savoy, Massachusetts, and the green mountains and farms in Vermont. These ventures require more stories, and I will follow up on them.

During the summer of 1950, I returned to the cave at Cole Mountain. None of my friends were around, so I went alone. I did not realize the potential hazards of going alone and my ignorance was nearly catastrophic! I had another year under my belt and I was slightly taller, heavier, and more muscular than my previous trip there.

I was well equipped with rope, flashlight, and a lantern (something we neglected to have last year). I felt comfortable. As I approached the cave opening, everything looked just as it was last year, with only small amounts of growth around the hole.

I lit the lantern and sent it down with my rope. I went down feet first, sliding into the hole. As I did, I had to squeeze and adjust my upper torso and arms to fully enter. When I approached the bottom of the hole, I was excited to see the room in the lantern's light and was careful not to knock the lantern over. The lantern was perfect, providing more visibility than we had last year. If I was going to find any treasures, it provided a much better chance of finding something in the room. The hoped for gold, obviously, was not there! After a complete inspection of the room and with no valuables discovered, I decided that it was time to leave.

Turning on my flashlight, I pointed it at the opening and panicked when I saw that the hole seemed smaller than before. I thought that the surrounding rocks had slipped and caused the hole to become smaller. I took a couple of deep breaths, assessed the situation, and climbed higher toward the top.

My shirt kept catching on the sides of the hole and I was sweating considerably. The sweat helped lubricate my body in contact with the rocks. When I was at the top, I stretched my arms through the opening, tilting my torso so that I had a smaller approach to exit the hole. I used my arms to lift me upward. That worked. Relieved, minor scratches, and a little worse for wear, I was out!

I sat on the nearest rock to catch my breath and felt relief at my near disaster. I vowed not to tell anyone about the close call! Like most kids, I quickly forgot about the potential bad ending and decided to go home.

I never returned to the cave.

CHAPTER 6

Mount Greylock Beckons:
Times of Change

During the 1950s, we hiked along the many trails of Mount Greylock and it happened with little or no planning. We would just decide to go. We usually chose two trails that were on the eastern slope. They were the Thunderbolt Ski trail and the Landslide trail and were the most convenient and nearest to our home. During the early 1950s, residents awoke to a new landslide that occurred on the eastern slope of the mountain near the original landslide. It now provided expert-level rock climbing.

The Thunderbolt Trail

The Thunderbolt Ski trail was built as an expert ski trail for the Williams College ski team in the 1930s. Just hiking the trail gave you reason to believe many a skier had taken some nasty falls on those switchbacks. Coming down the trail was just as difficult as going up. Most switchbacks were nearly straight down. The trail's life span was short, and with the trail being on the eastern slope, the early morning sun quickly melted the snow. There was no way that it would be feasible to use snow guns or to get grooming machinery down the trail for maintaining the slopes. The trail closed by the time we moved to the farm. But for us, it was a great hiking experience. An additional benefit to us was that in inclement weather, since we couldn't possibly get lost. Still, there was the possibility of accidently sliding on those slippery inclines! We never did get hurt though, but there was no question that at times we were out of control.

The Landslide Trail

There were more thrills and dangers climbing the Landscape trail rather than the ski trail. At times, there was no way but up! Our skills were challenged whenever we chose it. The trail demanded it! Our efforts required cliff and rock climbing and occasionally going around portions of the trail. This trail was challenging to say the least. We did not own nor were we familiar with using costly professional climbing tools. Sneakers or hunting boots were poor selections, but we could not have afforded these needed tools anyway. Bad weather made for slippery climbing, and on occasion, we would fall, slip, and skin our knees. We prevailed with the innocence of youth!

Occasionally we would be out fishing one of the remote streams and realize that we had a head start toward climbing the mountain. Relying on the slopes of the land was not a good substitute or safe. Just in case, we carried a magnetic compass so we would not lose our direction. Most of the time, the compass was as simple as one might get from a crackerjack box.

You can see the different activities and beautiful views of Mount Greylock on TripAdvisor's website. There are over 179 images are available for viewing (just click on the pictures to enlarge them). The images show monuments, signs, and other descriptions. You can expect many outstanding views of the mountain and the facilities there. Scenic driving tours and a roadmap are available via https:// berkshires.org/.

Greylock measures 3,410 feet and is the tallest mountain in Massachusetts. There are two paved roads that are used to access the top of the mountain. One comes from the south at Route 2 in Lanesboro and the second are local roads from Route7 in Williamstown. The road pull-off sites give beautiful views of the surrounding townships. Winter weather does sometimes limit access. There is a visitor gift shop and parking facilities near the top. There is a magnificent granite memorial tower approximately fifty-nine feet in height. The top of the monument has a bright glass beacon that is lit with electricity (at night). To save on costs, the electric lines were brought straight up the original landslide from the town of Adams. The tower provides views of seven local states when clear weather prevails. The ski and walking trails are also popular for hiking. About twenty years ago, an additional landslide occurred and now provides expert mountain climbing trails. The original landslide also continues to provide hiking but with less danger.

My friends and I have taken many hikes to the summit of Mount Greylock. One adventurous week, we went up seven days in a row just for the heck of it. The local paper the *Berkshire Transcript* reported it as local news color as it was done during the coldest part of the winter. Those hikes had never involved gold mining. We definitely had gold fever. We set a date for our Cole Mountain hike.

CHAPTER 7

Boiling Sap for Maple Syrup + Sugar

During the 1950s, now with a full family of Shafers (Dad, Mom, myself, Mary, Ed, Fat, and John), we had many activities that kept us busy and productive on the farm.

Late February and March (adjusting to the daytime temperatures), we had a lot of farm activities, such as producing maple syrup from the maple trees on our land. Although we only had six very large maple trees and several smaller ones, the production of sap was strong and consistent. We were able to gather a whole lot of sap, and that was critical because it took about thirty to thirty-two gallons of sap to make one gallon of maple syrup!

To obtain the sap from the trees, we had to learn how to make what were called taps from tree limbs. The limbs had to be about 1.5 inches in diameter and we had to cut them to about eight inches in length. We had to account for about thirty-two sticks formed into useable spouts. Because of the great amount of activity involved, we spread the overall time and effort throughout a couple of years.

Brother Ed and I, using a hand drill and a ¾-inch drill bit, bored a hole through the soft core of our sticks. I then used my pocketknife to slice about an inch of the bark from one end of the stick, tapering the end of it from an inch to three quarters of an inch. Then we used the hand drill with the ¾-inch bit to drill about three inches into the tree we were tapping. A spout on the unmarked end of the stick was then cut to bring about a usable spigot. We then inserted the ¾-inch round end of the tap into the tree. Grandpa and Dad supervised the whole activity. We continued the same activity of four spouts per tree placed in a circle around the tree trunk for productivity. We hung a one-gallon bucket to each spout and continued to do the same preparations for the rest of our maple trees (two buckets for the smaller trees). Now all we needed was a large metal tub, lots of firewood, a large stirring spoon, patience, and a hot fire! We utilized Mom's paring jars for the final product.

One year, when we were getting lazy, we decided to use the stove in the kitchen to boil the sap. We decided that since the sap flow was slow, but we had no idea of the problems we would have. The vapor from the boiling sap caused the glue on all the furniture to loosen. The wallpaper on the walls also peeled and hung loose. We had more work to do. We never thought of that and never did that again!

CHAPTER 8

Blackie: My Pet Crow

T hings were going well with our family. I had reached the ripe old age of fourteen. I was the eldest of the children in our family and was expected to do many of the chores at the farm. Dad was working in the northern part of Adams, at the Limestone Company. He delivered fifty-pound bags of powdered limestone with his Diamond T flatbed truck to both local and state-wide farmers. I went on trips with Dad and sat in his lap. I would steer the truck's huge steering wheel and operate the push-button gears.

Mom was working for Sprague Electric Company in North Adams, Massachusetts. Her job was soldering steel capacitor leads to electronic capacitors on their production line. Her income was very modest, and within a ten-year span, she retired from Sprague.

She received a weekly pay of $15. Mom was very prompt in using $2 a week for gasoline and $10 a week for groceries at George's Supermarket. When Dad went a long trip, I would use some gas from Dad's truck by siphoning it with a plastic hose. Many times, I drank a whole lot of gasoline. (Yuck! Maybe that's why my teeth were so soft.)

I, of course being fifteen years old, spent a lot of time at our farm doing the chores. My main chore was mowing our lawns and then trimming the weeds around the farm and our home, which were requirements. Dad taught me to use a pair of sheep shearing scissors to trim the weeds. These shears were difficult to manage for my small hands. So I said to myself, "There's got to be a better way!" I thought for a moment and came up with an idea. "Use the small electric fan to cut the weeds." The fan's blades cooled us during the warm weather while rocking on the porch. Because it was small, I was able to mount the fan on a broomstick. This made it easier than having to bend over when cutting the weeds. It gave me the ability to swing an arc with both of my arms to give the blades of the fan a far better cutting action. I connected the AC cord to an outlet on the porch and tied the other end of the cord to the top of the broom handle. This contraption was what we would call a weed wacker today! Unfortunately, I was unaware that if I had only known about copyright laws, I might have become richer!

While I was cutting the lawn and weeds, I could not help but notice that there were several crows making a lot of noise across West Road. Thinking that it was rather strange, I crossed the road and went up the hill to a group of pine trees on the hillside. That's where the crows were making such a fuss. It turned out that two crows were protecting their nest of babies at the top of one of the trees. The tree was more than fifty feet tall and was massive, to say the least.

I had been very jealous of my friend Ed who had captured a gray squirrel in a wooded area near his home and had brought the squirrel home as a pet. He placed the squirrel in a large cage and proudly displayed the squirrel to me. So why couldn't I do the same thing with a baby crow? Then I would have a pet that surely would be as good a pet as Ed's squirrel!

I looked up the tree with earnest and sought a way of climbing the limbs to the nest. It was quite a tricky maneuver making the climb. I was successful and I got a good glimpse of the baby crows. They were nearly full feathered and appeared ready to fly. There were three baby crows that were obviously hungry and continued to call for food. One of the parent crows came near and watched closely to see who and what I was. I carefully cradled one of the baby crows in my hand and put it in my jacket pocket. That left two more babies in the nest, so I said to myself, "I should only take one!" The nearby crow seemed not to notice, and I felt it was better not to alarm the parent crows any more than I already had. I proceeded down the tree and quickly brought the baby into our barn and placed it into one of our rabbit cages. I felt good about leaving the parent crow with two babies. I brought water and chicken feed for the new baby and hand-fed him until he was satisfied. I couldn't wait to tell Ed about my new pal.

I named the crow "Blackie." In a short period, he had all of his feathers and indeed was a very handsome guy. He grew quickly to his full body potential. He had two chicken feed (corn) meals a day and an occasion slice of bread, which he really seemed to like.

His wing feathers quickly needed trimming to limit his flying distance. I carefully cut several of his outer wing feathers with a pair of scissors. He was able to fly a short distance and seemed as though he was happy to jump onto my arm and shoulder to rest. I no longer had to trim his feathers. He was more comfortable balanced on my right shoulder. Blackie loved riding with me down our road. The wind from the speed of the bicycle made his wings and body shake. Those who saw Blackie riding with me were amazed.

Dad took a liking to Blackie. He would take Blackie to the local tavern, which was called the Commercial Street Cafe. Dad enjoyed the pub's draft beer with a whiskey chaser on a regular basis. Dad put Blackie on the bar. Soon Blackie found the whiskey glass and proceeded to have his own whiskey. The bartender renewed the shot glass full of whiskey several times. Blackie would shake his head and splatter the whiskey all over the place. He was definitely drunk and messed a white splat on the bar. The bartender quickly cleaned it up with a wet bar cloth so as to ensure the cleanliness previously there. The patrons of the bar found the entertainment hilarious. Dad would take him home to me when I returned from work. Can you imagine what trouble with the authorities that the bar owner and the establishment would be in today if they allowed the crow to be there?

I enjoyed Blackie until I joined the US Air Force in 1958. In the early spring of 1959, my brother John told me that Blackie had drowned when he had fallen through the thin ice for a drink of water from our dam.

I think about him often even to this day. It is now 2018 and every day I see at least two crows eating bread we had placed on the railing of our wooden deck, behind our house, in New York. They fill their beaks with bread, go to the water dish, soften the crumbs of bread by dipping their beaks full of bread, fly off, and feed their off-spring in the nearby trees in our backyard. At times, they leave their white blobs both on the deck and on our driveway. A full-pressure water hose becomes a necessary item at this time.

CHAPTER 9

New Experiences: Intro to Hunting with Dad and Friends

The next phase of my life was new and exciting—hunting. The first thing my dad introduced me to was his hunting club, the Adams Sportsmen's Club. I attended several meetings there and I felt that I was in seventh heaven! The second meeting there, I was chosen by the members to attend a sporting camp activity sponsored by the Federation of Fish and Gun Clubs. I would interact with about fifty attendees. We were housed in small cabins, with upper and lower bunk beds, for a solid week. The gun club sported the costs. I only had to promise that I would give a report of the activities at the next meeting.

At the camp, I was introduced to shooting at paper targets with .22-caliber rimfire rifles, shooting with 20-gauge shotguns at clay pigeons thrown downrange by hand-operated clay pigeon throwers, and shooting with bow and arrows at larger targets, all of which were on safe and reasonable distances. Of course, we all ended up as experts, right? We trapped for small animals in the woods and with expert advice mounted them for display. Maybe one or more of us would end up to be taxidermists! Safety lectures and demos introduced safety while hunting.

Dad gave me his double-barrel 12-gauge shotgun. I obtained my hunting license and we soon were hunting snowshoe rabbits in the Savoy forests. Dad had a bluetick hound and a beagle. The bluetick was bigger and taller than the beagle. He was about sixteen inches tall and good for deep snow, while the beagle was only twelve inches tall but had a great bellowing voice compared to his brother hound. Sometimes the bluetick would decide he liked deer better than rabbits and take off running the deer instead of a rabbit. When that happened, the deer would take off running a pretty straight direction to some unknown part of the forest and the dog would take all day to come back! The beagle was then the only dog we could count on to hunt for more rabbits. Sometimes that would take a long time, and at times, we left him there and came back later that day to see if he had come back. When we went home for dinner, Dad would leave his hunting jacket, along with a couple of treats on the snow. This was encouragement for our hound to lie down on Dad's jacket when he returned from his romp. Dad's smell, from wearing the coat during the day, would encourage the dog to do that and wait for our return. He always came back!

Dad taught me that the rabbit always ran in a counterclockwise circle and usually came back to almost exactly where the rabbit had been jumped by the dogs. My first chance to bag a snowshoe was successful. Dad also bagged one. When we got home, the first thing we did was clean the rabbits and prepare them for the freezer in the house. Mom cooked rabbit stew (hasenpfeffer) often. Rabbit hunting was exciting and we went almost every weekend during the winter season.

Above picture is of a snowshoe rabbit. They weigh around four to five pounds. Originally this species came from Canada, but the Adams Sportsmen's Club stocked them in our area. The photo below is of a whitetail deer.

That experience made me want to have a new shotgun for pheasant and rabbits and a rifle suitable for deer. I purchased a .30-30-caliber Winchester lever action from Russell Sturtevant for $40 and an Ithaca 12-gauge pump shotgun for $95 from Strauss Auto Stores. Money just flies, doesn't it?

Deer Hunting with Dad

My deer rifle was about to get used for what I bought it for, deer hunting of course. Dad and I decided to go deer hunting in Vermont. Deer were more plentiful there than in the more populated Massachusetts. Dad had just purchased a red-colored four-wheel 1957 Ford Bronco and it was ideal for hunting purposes. Dad said that he would use his 12-gauge shotgun and added, "You will have a better chance with your rifle." We stopped at the Vermont border and purchased their hunting license in a hardware store at $12.50 each. I was glad to start hunting in Vermont. We could not use my rifle for hunting deer in Massachusetts because Massachusetts law allowed only shotguns for that. It was fine to use shotguns for small game and deer though.

We got up early and proceeded to go where Dad knew a good place for deer hunting, near the Vermont border. It was a cold day to hunt and we had bundled up with our red Woolrich hats, jackets, and pants clothing and Timberline hunting boots. The snow, glaring from the sun, was very bright, so we brought our sunglasses and our binoculars too. The horns on buck had to be more than three inches in length. Special permits for hunting doe were sold only to resident Vermont hunters.

When we arrived at our hunting destination, I started up the trail that was cut some day in the past by a woodsman cutting lumber. Dad proceeded to the top of the hill, and I perched on a rocky ledge near the top. I was settled in for about an hour when a small deer came by my stand. It was a tiny baby by most standards, so I waited for it to pass, thinking that a larger deer could also be passing by any time. I sat for a long time waiting. I did hear a shot that was nearby, but I did not know the exact location that Dad had gone to, so I just waited. The snow was deep and cold, and after several hours, I went back to the Bronco. Dad was there and with a smug grin, as he sat smoking his cigarette, said, "Where's your deer?" I assumed that Dad thought I was the one firing my rifle. He laughed and said, "I could have used your help!" Lying behind the Bronco was a nice-sized buck with several points on both antlers. Dad was tired from dragging the deer and said, "Let's get this loaded and head for home!" I was disappointed, but glad for Dad. I said, "Next time it will be my turn!" We went home and hung the deer in the barn. We were going to hang it for a few days and let the deer bleed out and after that prepare it for butchering. We had plenty of venison for this season. The next year, we would go to the green mountains and Hicksey's farm where we knew they allowed hunters and there were plenty of deer. (The deer population was overeating his pasture.) Dad purchased a twelve-foot trailer and hitched it to the Bronco for the trip. It was quite a long trip away.

*****

I had recently returned home from the US Air Force after serving for four years. I returned in 1963 and worked in North Adams at a television repair shop. My electronics training in the US Air Force and the job in Crestview, Florida, at a television repair shop gave me enough background to repair televisions and install antenna systems on rooftops in the North Adams and Adams area. My insurance agent came by when I was on an especially steep slate rooftop and yelled, "Hey, Bob, please be careful up there!"

Work was slow in the television business there, so I applied at GE in Pittsfield, Massachusetts, and landed a job working on Polaris Guidance Capsules in the navy building off Route 8. We were living at the Willows motel with relatives. Because it was quite a distance to the GE position, I moved from Williamstown, Massachusetts, along with my family to nearby Dalton, Massachusetts, where we had purchased a home. To augment our income and help to pay for our home, we applied at a motel in Lanesboro as clerical help handling guests. Shortly after that, I was laid off from the navy job and applied for work in the instrument repair shop just up the road and was accepted. I worked there for about a year and got bumped by a technician who was union and capable of doing my job in the repair shop.

My boss at GE, who was named Leonard, was disappointed in losing me and asked me into his office. He told me that IBM was hiring in the Poughkeepsie and East Fishkill area. They were in need of technicians. That year, he had met a man also named Leonard at an electronics show and said he would contact him and make an appointment for me to see him. He did, and with my ego bolstered, I went the next Monday to apply. I drove down to Poughkeepsie, taking the Taconic south turned east on Route 44. Shortly, I came to a medium-sized building with an IBM sign on it. I stopped, went in, and asked for Mr. Leonard and told them I had an appointment. It turned out that there was a huge IBM plant in Poughkeepsie just off Route 9 where they had a lab facility for Instrument Services.

The building on Route 55 was an office building only. There was some confusion but eventually I did get the interview with a fellow called Tilghman who was to be the manager of the instrument repair shop in the new East Fishkill plant. We discussed the job, pay offer, location, and type of instrumentation that I had some experience with. He was interested in the fact that I had worked on Dymec instrumentation. I returned home and waited for his call because he wanted to talk to his boss about me. Several days later, I got a call from the personnel department asking about my interest level. He said that the pay level at $105 was good. What did I think? Well, I said, "It may sound good to you, but Mr. Tilghman had offered me $115!" A second call from him confirmed the offer and I had the job! Well, it was good and after two years, I got a $5 boost! That started my career for thirty years. Little did I know then that the Dymec instrumentation that I was familiar with was only a multimeter. The equipment that was in question was a full room of very special high-frequency (GHz) equipment!

We found a new home in Worley Homes in Hopewell Junction, New York. After explaining to the owner, Tex Worley, that I did not have that kind of money, thanked him, and started to leave, Tex said, "Wait a minute. What if I loaned you the $4,500?" We purchased our home for $14,000. We moved in the next week. IBM covered the cost of the moving van from Dalton, Massachusetts. We had a big "moving in" party and that is where I met my friend Mike.

Mike came as a guest in our camp. We had driven three hours during the afternoon before deer season started and stopped at a general store on the Vermont border to purchase our Vermont hunting licenses. We had brought a lot of gear with us that we would need to make the hunt successful. Our destination was Hicksey's farm several miles into Vermont. That year, I carried my Winchester 30-30. Mike brought his Savage 30-caliber bolt action. It had become traditional that we stop on Route 22, at the inn with a mounted and stuffed rabbit with deer horns that were screwed into the rabbit's head and placed above the bar. It was quite a busy place. And when we arrived, it was apparent that Dad had been at the bar ahead of us. He was definitely under the weather. Dad was arguing with the barkeep that someone had stolen his $5 bill that he had left on the bar when he decided that he must go to the men's room! Our arrival was timely because the locals were getting pretty upset. But with the two of us arriving, they were indeed overmatched. After one more round of beer, we settled with the barkeep as we left and proceeded to the trailer at Hicksey's farm, which was just a short distance across the state line.

Dad and my brother John had previously driven to Hicksey's farm and had set up the trailer in our parking area. When we arrived at the campsite, we discussed the layout of the land. We set the time that we would awaken, chose our sleeping quarters and placed our outfits, ammo, and rifles next to our bunks so that there would be no confusion and went to sleep until the legal time for hunting approached. We were off to the races at dawn.

In the morning, Mike decided that he would go to the top of the hill behind the trailer. It was quite open and had a long range down the slope. There were deer trails around the perimeter. John and I went down the other side of the road and set up along obvious deer trails present there and patiently waited. I moved a little and scared a buck that had been lying down nearby and he headed in a hurry down the hill from me. I yelled to John, "He's got horns!" I quickly raised my rifle and pointed it at the deer levering three quick shots in the direction the deer was running. I was lucky and bagged the deer and it went down. I approached and fired an extra shot into the neck so that he would not suffer. We gutted the deer and dragged it to the trailer. While we were getting to the trailer, we heard a shot from the hillside that sounded as though it might have been Mike shooting. It was. Well after the shot, out of breath, Mike arrived at the trailer. He had been rapidly jumping down the stream near the hill. Using a cigarette, because he knew his cigarette was three inches long, he quickly measured the horns. They were only about two and a half inches long. Mike knew that there were locals driving slowly on the nearby road, obviously monitoring the hunters in the area, and panicked and took off for the trailer. As it was, he was right. While we were at the trailer, two locals who said they were fish and game officials entered our campsite. They had the deer that Mike had shot on the back of their pickup truck. They talked about how the horns were obviously short and it was too bad because it really was a nice deer. They might have forgiven any hunter who had made such a long shot and miscalculated. We told them that we were deputy sheriffs with our gun club in Hopewell Junction and we would keep a look out for any potential poachers. Mike showed them his badge. In the meantime, they were still looking at our boot markings in the snow. They left, indicating that the deer would be donated to a local butcher.

I had earlier suggested to Mike that he wear new boots with large markings on the soles. I told him that I had an extra pair of boots that he, just in case, should wear. The soles on my old boots were worn thin. He agreed and proceeded to put them on and then messed up his previous tracks around the trailer area. Mike was happy he had changed his boots! On the way home, we talked about the close call!

We still had a lot of hunting left on rented gun club properties in the Hopewell Junction area plus our own hunting preserve lands.

Deer Hunting in Dutchess County

When Mike and I returned to Dutchess County from our camp in Schoharie County, we had many opportunities to hunt deer on land either owned or leased by Whortlekill Rod and Gun Club. The hunting season in the southern tier of Dutchess County was upon us. The properties that we could hunt on were many. The cabin in Schoharie would be used by us in the next year's deer season. We did continue some hunting in the northern part of New York when the upstate counties opened their season for deer hunting.

I have a picture on the wall of my office in my basement depicting me sleeping against a large maple tree wearing my hunting clothes, my trusty Ithaca pump shotgun lying nearby, while a big buck deer passes me by with his tail waving in the air! An artist by the name of Jack Lasherway painted that picture with the buck deer slipping away. He had painted caricatures of the deer on the clouds above me and a gray squirrel nearby. I only paid $35 for the picture. I am sure it is worth much more now than then. It certainly is to me.

The only difference between hunting at Vermont and at Hicksey's farm was that we had to use 20-gauge to 12-gauge shotguns for any hunting in our area. Neither of us had a pistol at the time and no rifles of any caliber were allowed that qualified for deer hunting.

There was one special opportunity that I owned a 40-caliber single-shot black powder rifle, mostly as wall decor. Mike continued to use his 20-gauge bolt action. We had many places to hunt and could hunt straight from our home to nearby locations in Hopewell Junction or other nearby towns. I only used the black powder rifle once. I used my Ithaca 12-gauge pump that gave me five rounds in the chamber.

One area that had many deer trails and seemed likely to be a good place for hunting deer was on state property near Pawling, New York. Mike and I had scouted the area on the first day before deer season in New York. We hiked to the top of the mountain to some rocky ledges where we positioned ourselves, looking down into the valley below, to watch for any deer, especially bucks. We were just several hundred feet away from each other. The distance below us was considerable. We could hear deer milling around and splashing through some loose water puddles about a couple of hundred feet out of sight from us. They continued playing around and we were anxious to see the deer. We kept hearing them get closer. They just never seemed to come out of the small area that was just out of our sight. Every now and then, as darkness got closer, we would get slight glimpses of deer just near the edge of the brush.

All of a sudden, I saw a rather large deer nearer to the hillside approaching me. He was quite a way off yet, and he kept hiding behind some large boulders at the bottom of the slope, so I waited patiently. If I shot too soon, I was sure to miss. Not that it would be a long shot, it would have been nearly straight down at him, but I could only get glimpses of his upper body. I waited until I could see his full neck and his shoulders. I got anxious and pointed my shotgun strait toward his neck. Because of the downward angle, my shot went high and actually missed. I racked in a second shot and fired again. This time, I thought I had hit him in the neck, but as it was, I only slightly grazed his neck, just under his eye. Another miss! The deer was startled and headed down the hill back to the brush. I fired the third shot and hit him directly in the neck. He fell and thrashed about. It had been a difficult shot and I hurried down the slope to get closer. It would have been impossible to fire until I could get closer. He stopped thrashing about as I got close. I fired another shot at the back of his head and he fell down for good.

I waited for Mike to come down the hillside and assist me in dragging the deer up the slope. In the meantime, I started to cut the deer so as to remove the intestines. By the time Mike got there, I had cut the guts from the deer. Mike said, "Wow, what a big deer that is!" We took a rope and put it around his neck and front legs. The deer was indeed not only big but also very heavy. By this time, we were both tired. Mike, who still smoked, said, "Let's hold off until I get my breath!" It was just about dusk when we attempted to drag the deer up the hillside. We just could not do it. We finally decided to drag it parallel to the ridge and went south to the road. Just as we got to what was an opening in the upper ridge, Mike slipped and fell. It was really a bad fall. He had broken or at least injured his ankle. I told him to go to the truck and find a better trail for us to get there. In the meantime, I used the rope around a tree to pull the deer to the top. Mike came limping back and had a flashlight to guide us back to the truck.

That incident put Mike out of commission for several weeks. I drove the truck home and we put the deer in Mike's garage. We hung the deer in an eight by twelve rafter at the top of the garage ceiling. A couple of days later, a member of our club helped to take the skin off the deer, and we sawed the rack off. It was a full eight pointer. Mike and I and Richard helped cut up the venison to put it in the freezer.

We never hunted that area again until the following year. We did take advantage of other leased assets held by the gun club. The only thing that had happened was that when Mike was ready to shoot what he thought was a deer, it was a huge buffalo. The owner had the biggest herd this side of the Mississippi. Mike got out of the buffalo's environment and we headed for the gun club after the owner cooked us some bison steak!

This deer would weigh in at about 150 pounds. It took me many years of hunting to finally get one this large. But that is for another story.

CHAPTER 10

Hunting in Schoharie County at Our Club's Campsite

During the early years of the 1980s, our gun club purchased a six-acre plot of land, with a small cabin on it, located in Schoharie County, New York. The location was adjacent to the four-thousand-acre state land that was open to hunting. Mike and I presented the initial proposal to purchase the land to the board of directors. The price had been negotiated to around $14,000 by one of the board members who dabbled in real estate and had already seen the property. The board of directors voted in favor as they liked the thought of purchasing a small parcel. The club hadn't purchased any land in years, and they felt this would be the best way to approach continued purchases. The purchase then needed approval from the general membership meeting set especially for this purpose. Many regular members investigated the property in anticipation of a hard vote.

The theory, explained to the members, was to purchase small parcels of land, near state land, with a dwelling and at a relatively low price, especially if we purchased with cash. Purchasing larger acreage parcels tended to limit the club to hunting that location and would require more cost associated with taxes and maintenance. The costs are compounded with a dwelling located on it and the possibility of requiring a mortgage to purchase the property.

Using this theory, we might be able to purchase several small parcels, minimize cost, and give us more flexibility for hunting different locations. This sat well with the members at the special meeting and approval was obtained.

The property had a rugged driveway but a four-wheel-drive vehicle could enter with some difficulty. The cabin was quite old, but comfortable. It had a small kitchen, with a sink, table, chairs, and a gas stove for cooking. The main room or living room was about twelve feet deep by twenty-four feet in width. The only furniture in the larger room was a cot-style couch that opened into a bed. There was also a rickety pot belly stove that had seen better days. It was usable though and we did use it the first year. Prior to the next gunning season, members of a work party did put in a new stove. It was mounted on a cement slab in the center of the room near the far wall. It worked to perfection. There was no heat like the heat you get from a potbellied stove when it is frill of firewood and properly stoked. The new stove was slightly smaller than the old one but was very efficient.

During these work parties, there were other projects to make the cabin more accessible, livable, and weathertight. It is amazing how our club members could make projects like these appear so easily. Many skilled members participated to accomplish these tasks. By taking part, members earned credit toward their yearly requirement for work hours. A partial list of the work accomplished at the initial workday outings is as follows:

- Replacing the gas lines to the propane tank from the tank to the stove
- Lugging the gas tanks to town to get them filled with propane (fifty-gallon tanks)
- Improving the driveway for easier access and the drainage past it
- Clearing of brush in the immediate area of the cabin to provide parking space
- Paint the window sashes and porch area
- Patch and tarring the roof surface
- Thoroughly cleaning the kitchen cabinets and the inside of the cabin
- Making the entrances more secure and putting in new doors with locks
- Cutting and stacking enough firewood for the upcoming season
- Ensuring the outhouse behind the cabin was serviceable (a dire necessity)

Over the years, work parties made many more improvements. These made the cabin more suitable and comfortable. Being the club's first outlying property with a cabin, this was heaven.

All of this led to the story of our first deer season at the camp.

Seven hunters were there for that first hunting trip to the camp. They included Mike, Michael, Freddie, Norm, Richard, Phil (a guest allowed by club rules), and myself (Bob).

The hunting season opened that year on a Monday and we arrived on Saturday. Since this was our first hunting trip there, it was thought best to arrive early. We had to set up camp and plan our hunting area. We arrived around noon and unloaded our gear and started to shape things up. Decisions had to be made as to where everything would go, who would sleep where, plan our meals, inventory our supplies, and all the other things that go with the first day of any outing. We reviewed contour maps, selected potential first-day sites, and relaxed with a few beers. We never mixed alcohol and hunting, but because we were not going hunting until Monday, why not? A nice comfortable fire was built in the potbellied stove.

Saturday evening was a time to relax and enjoy the company. Mike had prepared a meal of venison stew that he had brought with him, and we shared many stories over dinner. Afterward, several more beers, the warmth of the fire, and several long-winded stories were combined to make sure no one had any trouble falling asleep that evening.

Sunday morning, it was my turn to cook. Most had risen early or were encouraged out of bed. The smell of food won out. Everyone enjoyed a bacon and eggs breakfast. Everyone was anxious to get out into the woods, but a somewhat natural mess of the cabin had occurred during the past evening. Cleaning up is necessary for good camp discipline. Every one pitched in and after taking care of the cabin and other basic necessities proceeded to start our investigative forays into the woods. Most of the day, we hiked into and back from the locations we had selected for "eyes-on" recon, looking for deer trails, droppings, bedding areas, antler rubbings on brush or trees, feeding disturbances in the leaves, and sources of water. The location and direction of natural pathways and logging roads could also be important. Of course, the information gathered indicated where the deer have been and not necessarily where they are at the moment!

Deer are basically nocturnal creatures. Their visual acuity is far better than a human in lowlight conditions. Unless disturbed, they tend to have more movement during the night or the dawn and dusk periods of the day. What we've observed as deer sign generally is what was done during these times of the day. During the fall season, the rutting season causes deer to travel even during the day and this could also occur because of the disturbance of hunters passing nearby. Deer hunters who come in late in the day can make your day. The experienced hunter uses all of this information and knowledge gathered to select his actual hunting spot for a successful hunt.

Later, several of us went to town to restock some necessary provisions, like ice, beer, and some incidental groceries. We also needed to review the local roads and general surroundings and we did so. We stopped at the local bar, which was the only restaurant in town, and had lunch. The bartender was the owner and he filled us in on the local area. We talked about our place and just things in general. The bartender had told us that most of the locals depended a lot on the hunting season. It seems that most people here were on welfare and deer meat was the staple of most families during the cold days and nights of winter. He was very appreciative of our stopping by.

When we returned from our resupply mission, we proceeded to taste a few beers, just to "get the feel of things." The rest of the afternoon was just puttering around and we filled them in on what we had learned. They also told us about another recon that they had made of the area. We later had dinner. It was a sumptuous meal prepared by Chef Mike. After our feast, we proceeded to see if we could do more damage to the beer or maybe just a little of the wine that we had brought on the initial trip. This went on for a while, and we all swapped stories as there was no radio or television reception at the camp. We couldn't do this all night though, because our plans were to be up early and we needed a clear head in the morning. We also planned to be able to reach our selected locations well before the daybreak. With that in mind, we would retire early.

That day we had also met our neighbors who had the camp next door. There were three of them and they owned the cabin together. They planned to hunt only opening day and the weekends. We had little time to spend with them that day, but we promised to socialize more when they came back over the weekend.

Later that evening, we heard for the first time the mysterious sound that emanated from beneath the flooring! "Crunch! Crunch! Crunch!" It was very loud and made sleeping difficult as we were always waiting for it to reoccur. After a while though, it became strangely comforting!

The first day of hunting usually means that you just don't have time for breakfast, so you take something to eat with you. My choice was a couple of boiled eggs and a soda. Everyone dressed quickly, grabbed what they were going to take with them, and just sort of disappeared to their chosen location well before dawn. Everything important had been laid out neatly the night before. Necessary items like ammo, guns, compass, maps, knives, ropes for dragging, and anything else the members would want during the day were bulging out of their pockets or backpacks as they left.

Later trips were more successful. As we became better acquainted with the area, our success in bagging deer improved. Mike was probably more successful than any of us at this campsite. I remember him having taken several deer in the ensuing seasons. We had a great time there, but there were incidents that most likely should be told in another story!

The mystery surrounding "Crunch! Crunch! Crunch!" should take more than the first year's deer season at the cabin to solve. We had our suspicions, but couldn't absolutely be sure on this first visit to the cabin.

CHAPTER 11

Deception at Our Camp:
A True Story Filled with
Lasting Memories

This was our first hunting trip to our camp. Six hunters were in the group. Our lead camp cook was Mike, who as a wholesaler of combs and brushes, claimed to have sold Yul Brynner a Kent hairbrush. Michael, Mike's son, was on his first camp experience. Richard who worked in New York City with Mike was a born comic and always good for a laugh. In various scenarios, he and Mike had used Richard's similarity to famed singer Kenny Rogers in New York City gathering crowds. Fred was best described as an entrepreneur dabbling in anything from coins to real estate. Phil, Mike's brother-in-law, was on his first hunting trip with the group. Since I was born to a hunting family, I was right at home in this atmosphere. One of my hobbies was photography, so I brought my camera, which was very professional-looking, for the trip. All of us in a one-room cabin would certainly make for an interesting experience in this trip. The primitive facilities, lack of electricity, and no running water would surely test our mettle.

We arrived at noon (Saturday) in three vehicles. Mike took the lead and suggested sleeping arrangements and work assignments. The next priority was the unloading of our rifles, ammunition, extra clothing, socks, spare boots, water jugs, food supplies, lanterns, fuel, personal care items, beer, and wine. Each of us brought what they thought they would need for the entire stay. We completed an inventory when all of the items were in place to ensure we had thought of everything. Everyone certainly had big plans for a successful hunt as the combined ammunition on hand was enough to supply a marine combat patrol.

There were some items missing. We were short on water, beer, soda, paper towels, paper rolls for the outhouse, and a few cleaning supplies. A supply trip into town was necessary to acquire these items and anticipated resupply of necessities, like ice and beer. The camaraderie and habits of our group were such that you never could tell what might happen when gathered together, and beer was a definite necessity.

Using topographical maps, short forays, and our vehicles, we reconnoitered the surrounding acreage of state land, checking out roads, trails, streams, and ponds. Upon our return, we chopped wood, loaded the stove with firewood, tested our Coleman lantern's operation, replaced mantles and fuel as required, and made other minor preparations for our stay. Mike took his first turn at cooking dinner and prepared a spaghetti supper. Bob cleaned the dishes and Phil dried. All of us relaxed afterward with beer or wine and then settled in. The deer season would start Monday.

That night, it was a full moon. A rather large owl had begun hooting, "Hoot-hoot! Hoot-hoot!" on a nearby perch. A mysterious sound, "Crunch! Crunch! Crunch!" began under the flooring of the cabin and made sleep difficult. Both sounds felt ominous in the remote hunting location.

Mike and I drove into town Sunday to purchase the supplies necessary to complete the shortages our inventory had uncovered. Arriving just before twelve, we had time to kill. Since no one could purchase beer on Sunday before twelve o'clock in New York State, we decided to check out the local inn and eat lunch. The bartender and owner was a retired New York City cop and very talkative. Mike told him of his business in the city and we were instant friends.

He said, "I really appreciate the business. Practically everyone in this town is on welfare." We talked about the local hunting and told him of our recent purchase and whereabouts of our property.

Mike asked the proprietor, "Do you know the owners of the property adjacent to ours?"

"Three friends who only hunt opening day and weekends," he answered.

Now we had an idea of the number of hunters that would be in the area. We also knew that there was no chance that we would meet the neighbors before going into the woods. After lunch and obtaining the supplies with me driving and Mike observing, we made a further check on the roads near the camp looking for hunters preparing to hunt the area on opening day. Deer are nocturnal creatures and some hunter activity would help move the deer during the day. Returning from the trip, our newly purchased supplies were quickly loaded into the cabin.

It was dark before we knew it. Everyone in the group had by now returned to camp. Mike prepared a delicious venison stew for dinner made from last year's bounty. It was Fred and Michael's turn to do the dishes. Fully prepared and excited about the upcoming hunt, the group sacked in early.

The neighbors arrived late that night and we never got the chance to meet them that evening or even Monday. By the time we came out of the woods, they had already left.

All week we hunted from dawn to dusk, returning to camp weary and disappointed, no shots fired, no trophy acquired. Each day, necessitated by the close company of six grown men, everyone pitched in to clean up the cabin. Clothes were neatly set out for the next day's hunt. Lanterns were refueled and lit. The kitchen area and the main bunk room were swept of any litter or mud we may have dragged in. Empties and garbage were placed in bags and stored outside for disposal at the nearest dump area. Not having water or electricity, we did the best we could. Delicious and hearty meals prepared by our chefs were ravenously consumed. A few beers and storytelling rekindled our imagination and expectations. The potbellied stove erased the chill of the day. Each evening, we retired full and contented and each evening the ominous sounds returned.

Friday we learned that our neighbors had scored a trophy buck on opening day. Returning from his hunt, Mike heard the news. He had just met the neighbors. Jealous that he did not have a trophy deer to brag about, he decided to deceive the neighbors with the story about Richard. Sure he could pull it off, Mike bragged to the neighbors that an important guest member Kenny Rogers (Richard) would be arriving soon. Richard being a dead ringer for the singer Kenny Rogers made this an easy triumph. Mike knew Richard's full beard and hunting outfit would hide any misgivings. Adding the fact that his voice had similar characteristics to Kenny's just made it that much easier.

Posing as Kenny's agent, Mike announced that "Kenny Rogers" had arrived and I, as our club photographer, would be taking publicity photos for Kenny's next tour. Mike chuckled as the neighbors listened with obvious doubts.

Escorted by our group, "Kenny" made his appearance. I began taking pictures. Click! Click! Click! Entering the cabin and shaking hands with our new friends, Richard said, "Hello, I'm Kenny Rogers." The neighbors invited everyone to come in and visit for a while. Their cabin was newer and roomier than ours and it had a homey atmosphere. Many questions were routinely handled by Mike and Richard. During the conversations, Mike lavishly embellished his story by requesting discretion about Kenny's visit. Richard, terrific in portrayal of Kenny, followed Mike's lead and told of how his fans could be overwhelming. Beer and wine flowed freely. Photographing the neighbors with "Kenny," I ran out of film but continued "taking pictures" by discretely pressing the button on the flash unit.

One neighbor asked, "Hey, Kenny, did you bring your guitar?"

"No, I needed a break from my routine," said Richard.

Thank goodness no one asked him to sing! The discussion started to wind down. Richard finishing his drink said, "Sorry, I have to leave. I promised to call my office before nine. I'll be sure to autograph those pictures! Good night and good hunting!" There was no doubt they believed. Everyone said goodnight. The charade ended for the evening.

The following weekend, Richard presented the pictures complete with well-practiced forgeries. I discovered the source of the mysterious crunching sound under the floors. That source was raiding our garbage. When we heated the cabin, the heat made the pine boards under the flooring secrete pine tar. A family of porcupines moved in for the feast. When confronted, they left for greener pastures. The owl too moved on and was never heard again.

It was a new moon. There is nothing like being on post or at your stand as you greet the day. Everything slowly evolves. The light slowly increases. The day begins. The birds start chirping and may even investigate you as something that wasn't there yesterday. Suddenly there is a rustling through the leaves! Is it a deer? The tension mounts and you observe a squirrel or chipmunk nearby going about his business. Well, maybe next time, it will be a deer. As life slowly evolves, you really appreciate these early moments. Don't get me wrong, the rest of the day is satisfying, but there is something special about those early moments of the day.

Everyone hunted hard all day and came back with stories of whitetails flying over the place. We were sure that success was only a short time away. When our neighbors were leaving that evening, we wanted to hear how they fared that day. As it turned out, they had bagged a nice buck deer about five hundred feet behind our cabin. We had been unsuccessful Monday, and jealousy did creep in.

I don't remember anyone being successful in bagging a deer that year at or near the campsite. But I will say that the first weekend at the camp will be a lasting memory for all of us.

CHAPTER 12

My Favorite Teachers: Education at Adams Memorial High School

The draft was a near miss.

June 1957 at Adams Memorial High School for me was very easy. I wanted to have the least amount of schoolwork to allow me to work at jobs that I was involved in. I only had four study periods and five subjects (English, history, Latin, algebra, and trigonometry).

With Mary E. Malley (my English teacher) supporting me, I was the manager of the refreshment committee. My committee was responsible for distributing the goodies we sold to customers at the games for the gym, baseball, and football fields. I was responsible for cash dispersals, tickets for the games, soda, potato chips, and other refreshments. The committee members did most of the work!

As my English teacher, Mary, one of my favorite teachers, was also my supervisor for the committee. The last year of my education at Adams High was 1957, and I will tell you a couple of interesting interactions with her during her English class later in this chapter.

Other activities and jobs that kept me busy during the years of 1956–1957 include the following: Bienik's farm, Strauss stores, playground supervisor for the Fishkill Road Playground, odd jobs in manufacturing (cotton mill), and working in a different farm where I picked apples, made apple cider, hoed very long rows of cabbage and other vegetables, cleaned and maintained chicken coop, raised chickens, and egg production. The egg production was interesting. Just before Easter, we added metallic cobalt to the chicken feed. It changed the color of the eggshell to a blue color. We then would sell the eggs to the public as precolored Easter eggs.

Mr. Dubois, who not only was my history teacher but also was involved in the recreation department for the town of Adams, supported me as a playground supervisor. There I made parade costumes and officiated horseshoe tournaments, badminton contests, etc. Because I liked baseball, on my own, I coached a baseball team that was the same age as the local Little League players. I was fifteen years old and played Babe Ruth baseball at Renfrew field in the northern part of town.

My baseball team had parents with sons who actually played in Little League. One the parents of the Adams Little League, whose younger son played on my team, asked if I could have my team play their league champion team as practice for their upcoming tournament. I said, "Sure, but don't be surprised if we win!" We did! Can you imagine that?

During my senior year at Adams Memorial High in Adams, Massachusetts, I had the pleasure of being in Miss Malley's English class. When the school year first started, Miss Malley decided that after introductions, she would test the hearing of all my classmates, explaining that she wanted to know who could hear her speak. So she went through all the students with a whisper ("Can you hear me?"). Every student laughed when it was there turn.

She remarked, "I am serious. I am going to try this again. I am going to go through these words three times and lower my voice each time. If you can hear all three word phrases, please respond by raising your hand on each word phrase. Do not raise your hand if you did not hear me!"

Some of the students joked through the exercise but I took it very seriously, since I could not hear the last two. She repositioned my seating to the wall seats across the room. That was Miss Malley for you. She was like a built-in hearing aid!

Approximately halfway through the school year, Miss Malley gave out this assignment, "Write a story about any subject you have a great interest in." Wow! I jumped right on this one. I had just finished several science and sci-fi stories during the summer months. These stories included the United States absorbing many of the German scientists, Werner Von Brown as an example, and seizing many V1 and V2 rockets and their recorded data. Germany had also been the first country to build jet aircraft. These jets were seen by Allied and US Air Force pilots who were amazed that there was no propeller.

Use of the captured data and launch vehicles helped American scientists immensely.

I built my story on some of the early experiments of the now American scientists. There were some failures, but the United States had now built facilities to support missiles in the US inventory. Those missiles were the Atlas, Redstone, Titus, and Apollo spacecraft. The largest facility was Cape Canaveral in Florida at what became the Kennedy Space Center. Another was a West Coast facility in Pasadena, California, as a secondary lift off at the Space Control Operation in the Jet Propulsion Laboratory. This was mostly in case of bad weather at Cape Canaveral. Another facility was in Houston, Texas. It supported communications with the spacecraft and future space shuttles. Launches were primarily done in Florida.

When I was in the US Air Force at Eglin Air Force Base (AFB) in Florida, my cohorts and I were able to listen to most of the communications at the Electronics Building. We had to make sure that we did not interfere with Houston by accidently transmitting from our location.

Miss Malley read my story and was only somewhat impressed. I know because she only gave me a seventy-percentile credit! I had to read a portion of my manuscript to the class. I did get some oohh's and aahhs!

The last thing that I expected occurred during late in the school year. When our year-end grades were announced, Miss Malley read all the names but mine. It seemed that my written story must have had something to do with improving my English exam results, because at the very end, she congratulated me with a hundred percentile for my grade. Both she and my classmates clapped their hands in respect.

Miss Malley and Mr. William Dubois gave me many credits in their letters of support to our representative, in my quest to attend the Air Force Academy at Boulder, Colorado, in 1957. All my tests were sponsored by our senator from Pittsfield, Massachusetts. I went to a testing site in Burlington, Vermont, to prove my ability. Activities were mainly physical in nature and I excelled in that.

Unfortunately, I was not selected as a candidate for the first class to enter the Air Force Academy. I guess I was not as well-known as a politician since the slot went to a politician's son. Had I been selected, I would have been sent to Vietnam for combat after my training at the Air Force Academy. I heard that he had been shot down while flying a Phantom jet. The pilot ejected and he never recovered. I never did learn anything else.

With no other academy selection in mind, I decided to enlist in the regular US Air Force and soon would be in basic training at Lackland AFB in Texas.

I told my recruiter that I wanted to be an air policeman, but he said, "Well, son, you scored very high in electronics. We need your experience. Once out of basic training at Lackland AFB in Texas, you will go to Biloxi, Mississippi, where you will be schooled in basic electronics. Then your next assignment will be at Eglin AFB in Florida with further training in flight line maintenance."

In the dead of night, we were sent from Lackland AFB to Biloxi, Mississippi. We were told that a unit of the Air National Guard was being sent in for training, and our unit was trying to get into the school before the guard unit got there. They beat us to it.

While waiting, we went through advanced combat training, like wearing gas masks, entering a building and taking off our gas masks, machine guns firing live shells over us as we crawled under barbwire, rope climbing over high obstacles, and dropping to the other side. Most of us went into huge puddles at that point. We also took firearms training on the rifle range where I received an expert ribbon. We used M1 30-caliber Carbines left over from Korea.

While waiting for all of this to happen, I went to my commander and asked for assignment into di-di-dah school (SOS). My first stripe had relieved me of picking grass and stripping cigarette butts from the ground. I eventually got to twelve bits a minute at the SOS class, but got stalled when I was told I would have to use a typewriter!

Since I was a barracks chief, I could get any goof off to substitute for me in the Mess Hall. The chow was excellent there. Every weekend, we had huge barbecued steaks served on glass plates. I gained nearly thirty pounds. One time, two other airmen and I went to New Orleans to an army post that served us on metal serving trays. We also took several trips to New Orleans even though we were past our twenty-five-mile pass limit. We enjoyed activities on Bourbon Street, dances on trips on wooden paddle cruise ships on the Mississippi, and swimming at Lake Pontchartrain and enjoying the girls and the sunshine.

CHAPTER 13

US Air Force (1958–1960)

From 1956 to 1957, I joined the Civil Air Patrol (CAP) in North Adams with the intent to learn about flying, knowing that one year in CAP would guarantee me a Third Class stripe when enlisting in the USAF.

The CAP was located at North Adams Airport and was responsible for encouraging local youth, fifteen to eighteen years of age, into flying. It definitely was a military unit that could lead to enlistment into the USAF.

Prior to joining the CAP, several of my friends and I joined the Air Force's Air Plane Flash movement. Our position was located in the bell tower of the Adams' town hall. It was our responsibility to monitor enemy aircraft flying through the Berkshire Valley toward more valuable targets to our south. We were issued 12-power binoculars, a telephone, and identity cards of potential enemy and friendly aircraft. We were to ignore obvious local traffic of small airplanes like a Cessna.

If we spot an aircraft that was flying south and at high and sometimes low altitudes, we would set off the following action: immediately note the airplane's direction and altitude, pick up telephone and dial the operator, and declare the message, "Air Craft Flash!" Then we would give the aircraft's information such as its number, location, and direction. We might have been helpful on September 11th when the hijacked airplanes flew from airports like Logan International in

70

Boston and crashed into the World Trade Center Buildings in New York City. Unfortunately, that was quite a few years after the Air Craft Flash units were disbanded.

Lackland AFB: Four-Week Basic Training

On September 15, 1957, I was on my way to the Basic Military Training in Lackland AFB, Texas, via the local train in North Adams, heading to Bradley Field in Connecticut and embarking in Lackland AFB. My girlfriend missed the train, but her parents saw me off. At Bradley, we were taken by bus to our assigned aircraft—the Super Constellation, built by Boeing, a propeller-driven four-engine plane with a triple-tail configuration. We got our seat arrangements and were off to Lackland AFB. The Connie, as it was called, was a beautiful airplane, but in flight, it shook like the devil. There were many of us that needed a break immediately after arrival in Texas.

When going through the basic outfitting activities, our allotments included uniforms, boots, hats, socks, and underwear and a small allotment of cash for menial things like shampoo, toothpaste, soap, and a haircut. Getting a haircut was certainly different than in civilian life. The barber really enjoyed himself with the cuttings.

He took one look at me and said, "How would like it?"

Most of us just joked, "Short will be fine."

When he started on my then long hair had, he went straight down the middle then front to back. When he finished his first stripe, he had cut two inches wide and the hair inside of the stripe cut to one inch long. Then with a laugh, he continued until I was almost bald. Then the barber said, "That will be $1, please. Thank you!" By that time, I was just about flat broke. I had just enough money to call Mom and tell her that I got there safely and ask if she could help me out financially. She sent $20 by Federal Express. Thanks, Mom!

US Air Force 1958

After the first couple of weeks at Lackland AFB, we had some breaks on the weekends. I had great expectations about my potential.

One of the local merchants encouraged our platoon to have a picture taken for the homefolk, so of course I had to do it. The picture I have here is about *sixty years old* and it is pretty rough, but a little glue helped, though it could have been better. Other things could have caused more damage. But look at how wonderful it depicts Mom's boy! Maybe, DaVinci or some other Italian with a paintbrush could have done better. Who knows? Thanks for the $20, Mom. It went a long way!

Pictured above is me wearing my uniform in 1958.

Each airman was assigned to a bunk and received a blanket, sheet, and pillow. Each airman was given a chest where personal items were placed. Practically everybody purchased a miniature crystal radio that hung on a wire antenna and we listened to it before lights out. All our boots were placed in the chest along with the socks and a shoe brush. Spit shining became an art!

All the airmen saved up their pennies to get soap, toothpaste, and toothbrushes. As a one striper, I was assigned to the upstairs bunks. There was a lot of commotion, at times, since not all of us got along, and it was easy to be jealous of anyone who wanted their bunk moved around a little. When we became too noisy, the sergeant major from downstairs asked me what was going on. Naturally, I told him nothing.

Fallout for early marching came at sunrise. It was the same old routine. Our bathroom items were the necessities for the early time of day!

Four weeks of basic training at Lackland AFB went by quickly. Typical training, besides marching, included shooting at the firing range using the MIA, a short rifle with a 30-caliber ammo designed for use with pistols and not very powerful. The rifles were leftovers from the Korean War. (I did get a sharpshooter rating with it.) We were taught how to deal with tear gas. They were thrown on the floor of the gas chamber, and we were told to enter taking our gas masks off as we went in. The tear gas was very strong and kept us in tears.

Next, there was a 30 mm machine gun firing live ammo on top of us, while we crawled under barbed wire strung just above our nose. Then we climbed a twelve-foot-high wooden obstacles and climbed down the other side. Climb other obstacles with rope swings that you were supposed to swing and clear the mud holes on the other side. I am sure there were more exercises, but if they couldn't think of anything else, you went on long marches. Parades with dignitaries and some families watching were popular. The problem was the temperature. Because of high temperatures, more than one of our trainees would collapse during the exercise. Of course, we were expected to learn the marching chants led by the instructors, no matter what.

Keesler AFB Biloxi, Mississippi

We got an urgent message that we were going to Keesler AFB for electronics training early, after four weeks, to fill a necessary head count. Rumor had it that we would only need four weeks to complete our basic training at Keesler. We were told we would complete the rest of eight weeks of basic training there and then go through electronics training. Unfortunately, a National Guard unit had pulled some strings and made it impossible to complete the schedule. There was a twelve-week delay in the schedule to start electronics training. The other four weeks, we spent doing various chores. To rearrange the basic training schedule at Keesler, the basic training was changed to only four hours per day. We spent the rest of the day with the following duties: picking up cigarette butts, pulling grass weeds out of the cracks in the walkways, pulling KP, buffing the hallways, and cleaning our barracks. When we had arrived, I had received a barracks bay chief assignment because of my Third Class stripe. After the first time on KP, I decided that any goof off in my bay would pull KP instead of me. Believe me, it was not hard to find one. This was okay with the barracks chief who had two stripes. The next level was a three striper at command level. Each of us had lanyards on our dress blues that indicated our standing. Yellow lanyards were for my level (one stripe), red lanyards for the barracks level (two stripes), and white lanyards (three stripes) for the commander level.

I spoke with our squadron commander about doing something that always interested me and that was what we called di-di-dah or Morse code school. Training was in the afternoon, so that got me off the typical chores I mentioned earlier. All I had to do was report back to my commander and tell him how I was doing with the Morse code. I gave him good reports. After a few weeks, I had gone beyond the dit-dit-dit (S), dah-dah-dah (O), dit-dit-dit (S) or SOS and up to twelve words a minute. My commander was impressed. Unfortunately, the instructors tried to get me to do better by using old Underwood typewriters. In high school, I had taken a typewriter class (with twelve girls) using IBM Selectric typewriters with ball inserts, so it became much less desirable using the old Underwood typewriters. I then started to believe that being a radio operator was not in my future. I still gave my weekly reports.

After twelve weeks, electronics training began (October 1958–September 1959).

I don't recall much about classroom decor, but it was similar to being in high school. Information was done on chalkboards, flip charts, slideshows, and verbal instructions. Basic characteristics of electronic components were discussed daily.

Terminology was discussed. Really basic items like resistors, capacitors, transformers, wire sizes, tubes (yes, tubes) were either demonstrated or put up on the blackboard. RF transmitters and frequency distributions were demonstrated either with actual radio gear or with scientific charts. Building our own radio was encouraged.

At the time, the circuitry was very simple, instructors encouraged students in radio transmission/reception by demonstrating a quartz crystal kit wired to a small speaker and antenna. Students built their own and usually brought them to their room for nighttime listening. Radio waves were discussed and compared to the actual radio systems that were being installed in our aircraft. ARC 27, ARC 31, ARC 57 Collins radios were displayed and demonstrated. Instructors suggested what radio might be installed in T-33, T-37 such as the ARC-27 and the B-47 bomber would have an ARC-31 and a B-52A might have an ARC 57. Occasionally the instructor for the day might be an engineer who worked for the electronics companies. Eventually, repairs and instruction for actual repair/tuning on these types of radios were done in the Electronic Radio Buildings at the various airbases.

The bars in Biloxi and the Airmen's club were a beer drinker's paradise. The base would bring in many celebrities who sang and performed on weekends at the Airmen's club. About 3.2 percent beer was sold there for $0.50 a quart.

There were no restrictions except for a twenty-five-mile pass limit. That didn't stop many of the airmen trainees (out of uniform) from going to New Orleans to see the Mardi Gras. Tall glasses of piña colada at $1.75 were in vogue there, so was the excitement of Bourbon Street!

In New Orleans, where we often went, a couple of other guys and I took a ride in a stern-wheeler paddleboat and sailed on the Mississippi River, which was cheap and fun. It was a floating bar and dance boat with Dixieland music and a lot of pretty girls. We often went to Bourbon Street to listen to Louis Armstrong, otherwise known as Satchmo. He was a great musician, famous for his Dixieland style of jazz music, and owned his own bar on Bourbon Street. The best time to go is, and was, during the last three nights of lent (a Christian event) for the big parade starting on Canal Street and ending on Bourbon Street. Satchmo died on July 7, 1971.

In August 1960, I was awarded my next stripe after completing twelve weeks of technical training at Keesler AFB. With that second stripe on my shoulder, I would arrive at Eglin AFB as Airman Second Class.

Bus Ride to Eglin AFB, Florida

I arrived at the Valparaiso gate, three miles from Valparaiso, Florida, and from there to our barracks, where we would be issued assignments.

When we arrived from Keesler AFB, there was a total of eight airfields that supported the 3242nd. I do not know how active or to whom those airfields have been allocated over the years. I do know that Airfield #3 was where the B-25 bombers trained in 1944 for the bombing of Tokyo, Japan. B-25 bombers took off from the USS Hornet, an Essex-class ship, sailing in the Pacific Ocean during World War II. Limestone lines were laid across the runway at Airfield #3, spaced equally to the length of the carrier. The B-25 would sit at one end of the runway and go full throttle all the way to the other end where the pilot would pull back on the stick before crossing the line to fly off into the air. Those lines were 824 feet apart. They were successful after many takeoffs. Once accomplished, as an exercise, two B-25s flew off from the USS Hornet, to the surprise of the personnel onboard. Later sixteen airplanes were placed at the far end of the carrier, which used up some space, and would perform the takeoff, but needed to drop off anything they could to be able to make the flight. Additional weight also needed to be shed, because of the one-gallon gas cans, full of aviation gasoline, on board each plane. They even threw out the door gunner's guns to lighten the load. This effort succeeded and had to be done, because the ship had been discovered way before the original takeoff plan. All sixteen bombers did successfully fly off with no losses. Later in the war, the USS Hornet was lost at sea.

The B-25 bombers, using incendiary bombs, bombed the approaches and factories that were manufacturing war materials in Tokyo. The bombing caused a heck of a lot of fire damage to Japan's war efforts. When the aircraft had used up all the bombs, the B-25s headed for the China coast. Most of the aircraft and personnel made it safely to China.

Note that since I left the US Air Force, Eglin has changed tremendously in support groups and missions. Even the US Navy, US Army, and some Allies have training facilities there.

Types of Aircraft

There were a number of aircraft, ranging from bombers, fighters, trainers, passengers, to cargo planes, assigned to Eglin and we had special areas and base ops for this effort. The following are some of the planes:

- B-52A bombers. The B-52 models were new to the US Air Force.
- B-47 jet bombers. These were used for training and tech modifications.
- B-58 Hustler. These were supersonic 1,500+ mph jet bomber with a 2,000-mile service.
- B-17 bombers. These were being discontinued from service.
- B-25 Mitchell. These were the last B-25s to be decommissioned.
- F-86 Sabre, F-100 Super Saber, T-33 Trainer, F-4 Phantom supersonic fighter.
- F-105 Thunder Chief, F-104 Starfighter, F-102 Delta Dagger, F-101 Voodoo.
- C-47, C-54, DC-3, C-130, C-123 propeller aircraft.

Those last on the list were mostly cargo planes, but some were there for engineering upgrades of military equipment. The C-130 is a good example.

Now that you have been introduced to nearly every plane in service at Eglin, I will tell you of my observations of what I thought to be the most interesting projects applied to these airplanes. My intent is also to tell you of my work on the airplanes on the flight line and my activities in everyday work assignments.

On the top of the list is the B-52A. This plane arrived at Eglin ahead of me. It was huge by any standard. It was quite a showstopper. At the next air show, President Kennedy made an appearance and the base put on quite a show, mainly for him.

I was inside of one of the hangars nearest to our Electronics Building and knowing that Kennedy was coming and that he would tour the flight line, I knew he would go right past me. I had brought my 8 mm motion picture camera and awaited for him to pass by the hangar doors, which were partially open. After reviewing the entire flight line, he looped past the hangar and I used about three minutes of film with him riding in the back of his limousine with his hair blowing in the wind with the top down. I was amazed at the lack of security. I knew that this seemed strange, but I first thought was that if I were a risk, he could have been shot, not by me of course. How prophetic that in a very short while, he would be assassinated!

I still have a DVD recording of Kennedy's visit and review it occasionally.

When Kennedy arrived at the reviewing stand, an F-102A interceptor bomber came over the back of the Electronics Building. The F-102 was a huge fighter plane and was only about thirty feet above the building. The pilot pulled the stick back and, at full speed, went spinning ninety degrees straight up into the sky and directly over the bleachers. The sound was deafening! What a show he put on! When he was out of sight, our ears were still ringing. The next show was a B-52 bomb running over the near bombing range. There the crowd and Kennedy ensemble had a view of the big bomber dropping a hundred bombs at a hundred pounds each for about two miles. It was a show of strength.

That particular bomber was destined to be modified shortly after that. Our maintenance crew was complaining that the B-52 was too big to put in the hangar. Upon reflection, the crew was correct. Our designers asked a simple question—what would happen if they shortened the tail? Well, the maintenance crew removed ten feet off from the tip of the tail. The bomber could then fit through the hangar doors and could completely go inside. After a short test flight, it became apparent that the B-52 could fly very nicely without that ten-foot section.

Another interesting idea was being tested just a short distance from our Electronics Building. We could hear extreme gunfire at regular intervals. They were evaluating the use of Gatling guns fitted to a C-130 cargo plane. Two sets of guns two, 20 mm and two 40 mm, were to be installed on one side of the plane through two small doors. The original Gatling guns were used during the Civil War back about 1860 and usually about 30-caliber firing many as four hundred rounds per minute. The guns in our airships were to have much heavier ammo and capability, firing as many as 4,500 rounds a minute with devastating effect. Many versions of the Gatling guns were to be and are today placed on ships and many other military vehicles.

I reported daily at the Electronics Building at 8:00 a.m. There, our first sergeant gave us our schedules. Most days, I had to go to the motor pool and requisition a pickup truck for flight line duty. On occasion when a hurricane approached from the Gulf of Mexico, we would have special duties to accomplish. I was the driver of the pickup truck that I had requisitioned. My responsibility was to lead a work party of four airmen, whose job was to protect the very large windows across the front of our building from possible damage caused by any hurricane approaching the base.

Our task was to retrieve from the supply depot heavy metal window shutters and attach them to hooks on the side of the windows. This was no easy task. There were approximately thirty-six large windows on three floors of the building about four by twelve feet each. Each shutter was four inches wide and weighed in at about fifty pounds. The pickup could only hold ten shutters on each trip from the supply depot. The tires of the truck showed the weight and we had to go slow as to not lose a tire from the pressure. Using steel cables with pulleys attached to the sides of the windows, we had to muscle the panels into place. Occasionally if the weather was blustery, we had our hands full. Now you know why only the young guys were used for this duty! After the hurricane warning was repealed we had to take the shutters down and returned them back to the supply depot.

My regular schedule was to be available for radio checks for aircraft being used for pilots that were getting their flight hours in. This procedure was quite simple until the radio malfunctioned. Usually the maintenance personnel would know if the pilot had already flew in for the day and had reported in his log of any malfunction. This probably called for a replacement of the radio used by this aircraft.

I would go back to the supply depot and get the required radio. Otherwise the maintenance technician would tell me that the pilot was on his way and then I would perform the typical check. We had many T-33 trainer jets that were used for flying time and the test would be simple. I would just speak into the microphone a phrase like, "Radio Check Eglin," and usually some local base like MacDill AFB in Florida would respond. If I got no response or an unacceptable reception, I would check the antenna connection between the two halves of the aircraft mainframe. A lot of times, the connection might have been pulled free during maintenance on the engine. At times, the cable might actually have been damaged beyond quick repair, and the aircraft would have to be pulled off the flight line for further maintenance. If the radio was simply malfunctioning, I would have to go back to the stock room and get a replacement. Our pickup trucks were invaluable as the planes could be a long way from the electronics shop.

This procedure was basically how any radio check on the various radio systems in each of the different planes we were asked to check out was done. The difference was the type of radio like HF, VHF, or UHF. The difference in the removal of the radios in the larger planes was that they were generally pretty high off the ground and needed extra effort or manpower to get them to the repair shop. The B-47s and B-52s were examples of this.

In the afternoon, I would meet with my technical support, Civilian G-7 level, and with his oversight, we would repair or tune the radios sent to us by Maintenance. I was known for how well I was able to tune the tuners of the ARC-27 Collins radio. The ARC-27 was generally a 25-watt UHF transmitter, and with great care, I could increase the wattage to as much as forty to forty-seven watts of power. Many pilots appreciated the larger output and would echo their appreciation after return flights.

During the first suborbital space flights out of Cape Canaveral at Kennedy Space Center, some of our technicians and I were able to monitor the flight frequencies and conversations of the Houston Space Center with the Atlas rockets and space capsules in orbit through, but we were not authorized to transmit.

Unfortunately at Eglin, one sad occurrence involved the death of one of our pilots after relocating the remote UHF radio control from the center console to the left side of the cockpit. On a return flight, it was normal for the pilot to change flight frequencies to base control frequencies just before landing. The pilot suffered from vertigo when he leaned toward the control unit and flew the T-33 into the ground. After an investigation, the new placement of the control unit was rated poor. I still don't believe it ever went back to the original location. A short time later, my work evaluation recommended my promotion for a third stripe to Airman First Class. That month, I was awarded the promotion.

CHAPTER 14

US Military Service (1961–1962): My Last Two Years of Service

Driving to Visit Home

One of our airmen named John was on duty (a three-day work week) with the transient alert group. John knew that I had talked about going back to Massachusetts for a two-week vacation from the US Air Force. I had plenty of accrued leave time to go visit with my girlfriend and her parents Earl and Lucille. They lived in Williamstown, Massachusetts, in Berkshire County. Earl and Lucille ran a small inn on Route 7. Their daughter Kathy had just finished high school and lived at home. My mother and dad lived on our farm in Adams, Massachusetts, and I could visit with them. John asked if I would be interested in driving home with him and said that he would take his car, a 53 Studebaker, that needed a ring and valve job. He knew a mechanic who would repair his car, worked really cheap, and could handle the maintenance required on his car. He felt that it would not be a problem going to Massachusetts and then back to Pennsylvania, his hometown, and get his car repaired. And when it's time get back to Eglin AFB, he would come to Massachusetts, pick me up, and help him drive back to Eglin. He estimated using about four days of my leave to travel. So why not do it?

Off we went. It was February and we didn't count on the sixteen-inch snowstorm we would encounter on the way. Another minor issue we had was that he had guessed fifty weight oil would suffice. Well, it held up right to the last can. Unfortunately, the oil blew heavy smoke the whole trip! We were fortunate that the police were busy with traffic because of the snow.

John admitted that he had never driven in the snow, so it was up to me to drive the last half of the trip. I assured him that I could handle the snow. John was grateful that, if one lived in Berkshire, one could drive with expertise in snow, even if it was a little slower than we anticipated. We were fortunate that the snowplows along the way did a good job.

Pictured above is a B52 Stratofortress being climate tested at Eglin AFB.

Spent Time at Home on Leave

I spent some time while I was at home with the Shafer and Estes family. It was nothing spectacular, but it was nice seeing them all. Hunting for snowshoe rabbits with Dad in Savoy was fun. On another day, I talked with Earl about me possibly buying a car. Earl worked in a body shop and had a very good knowledge about used cars. I was enjoying the extra pay that I received when I got my promotion to Airman Third Class.

Both families were curious as to whether or not the question of getting married might be on the table. Well, both Kathy and I talked about it. I explained to them that I would need my operations officer's approval to get married. I would have to find housing off base, because there was no room at base housing at my rank level. The one advantage though was that I would indeed get a housing allotment due me by my rank.

I said, "I will be going back to Eglin in the next two days and I would know better when I look into that."

We Were on Our Way

Well, those two days went by quickly, and all of a sudden, we were on our way. John showed up with his Studebaker and had it all nice and clean. Lo and behold, the engine purred like a kitten. We reversed our travel direction and were back in time at Eglin to go to our work station. I went back to the barracks and continued my duties. Apparently, John did not.

There were two odd things that happened. First, John had arranged for his work schedule to be covered by his friends at transient alert. Second, my roommate had found the bottle of moonshine that I had left under the floor of my closet. I didn't even know he knew about it. My barracks chief had warned me of his bad attitude when he was assigned to my room. He had taken the bottle of moonshine with him on a wild trip to New Orleans. We found out he had a fight with a stranger he hardly knew. During the fight, he used a tire iron to hit him on the head and killed him.

My roommate never came back.

Now back to John. He went home to see his parents at their home in Pennsylvania. John went there to get his parents to recognize his relationship with his girlfriend. They absolutely said that there's no way would they allow him to continue his relationship with her. Due to religious reasons, they threw him out of the house and told him he could no longer be considered to be a member of the family.

John did not show up for duty for two weeks. His work schedule was handled by other personnel at transient alert, and a three-day schedule was logged in for John the entire time he had been gone. It became apparent that the base commander, whose chain of command had failed him, would have to take disciplinary action if John was not located immediately. After a search was conducted, John was found shot dead, apparently by suicide, in an apartment in Philadelphia. The base commander shut the whole base down for two weeks. No one was allowed to leave the base.

During February and March, I spent a good deal of my time in the Electronics Building. There I continued to be assisted by my mentor, a civilian mentioned earlier. He had a great deal of knowledge of which I absorbed as best I could. One day, he said, "Let's all listen to the space race on our Collins VHF radio! Houston will be on channel—" (Sorry, that was confidential at the time.) It was fascinating to listen to the chatter. Houston would send messages to the capsules in space whenever there was a capsule leaving orbit and heading for pickup in the Caribbean Sea. The Mercury capsule astronauts would reverse course, placing the space shield in the front with their intent to slow the speed of the capsule.

This was where the atmosphere was the thinnest, and the friction would cause the heat shield to actually burn and shedding sparks like a July 4th sparkler, except to a much greater degree. It was at this time that Houston got nervous and every minute or so would call on their radio, "Mercury, this is Houston. Do you copy?" with about thirty seconds for the spaceship to respond before another broadcast. They continued until finally from the capsule came the response, "Houston, this is Mercury. We copy." The whole world listened on the television sets across the globe! Houston became famous.

The capsule was lined with tiles that were glued in place, and there was always the fear that they could fall off the spacecraft and cause a catastrophic failure of the Mercury capsule. Very few tiles were lost but that must have been some kind of crazy glue! When the capsule finally broke through the atmosphere, the space capsule would free up the parachutes (there were three large chutes), and the capsule would float down until they were just above the water and then they would release the chutes. A US Navy Destroyer was always just a short time away. There was one capsule that sunk because of the turbulent sea. The astronauts just barely got free in time and returned shaking from the hazardous return to the destroyer on a Navy PT boat. The capsule was recovered after quite a long time under the sea. Before Project Mercury was complete, the United States had placed six men into space.

Project Mercury was followed by the Gemini and Apollo missions. Eventually, man went to the moon. There were quite a few flights to the Moon. One was nearly disastrous, but the rest were successful.

By mid-March of 1961, I made up my mind to follow through on going home and propose to Kathy. I went to my squadron supervisor and talked to him. He agreed that if I wanted to do this, then it would be okay with him. I was to go home, get married, and come back, while he would prepare the necessary papers for the allotment increase in pay and I could terminate living in my barracks when I return. Now all I had to do was to go ahead with it.

I purchased a ticket on a Greyhound bus in Valparaiso, Florida, to Albany, New York. I figured that I could hitch a ride back to Pittsfield, Massachusetts, and get someone to come and get me. I was dressed in Air Force blues on the trip. The Greyhound Cruiser was very comfortable, and my seat was located at the top level, which gave me a good view. When I arrived in Albany, I went over to the intersection at Route 20, which should give me a chance to get a good ride. When I went into the service, hitching a ride was very common. I soon found out that an airman in Blues and carrying a full duffle bag would not get me a quick pick up. Well, guess what?

Times had changed. After about an hour of no drivers paying any attention to me, a police cruiser came over and the officer asked me where I was going. He explained that it was not a good idea to hitchhike. He smiled and suggested that I go back to the bus terminal and get a ticket to Pittsfield. There was no, "Thanks for your service!" Today, thank goodness that is the normal reaction. I reluctantly did go back to the bus terminal and called Earl, who picked me up in Pittsfield and brought me to Williamstown. Oh well, what's another $20?

When all the excitement calmed down and the proposal accepted, I decided that I could extend my leave for two weeks, which would suffice to make all the arrangements for the wedding. The first thing that I needed was a car. I purchased a pink and black 1952 Ford four-door for a reasonable amount. I don't remember the actual price, but it was somewhere around $400. Arrangements were made to have the wedding service at Saint Thomas Aquinas Church in Adams where my mother attended mass. I had gone to Catechism classes there as a child.

Earl and Lucille Estes made arrangements to have the wedding reception at their home in Williamstown on a grassy acre behind the hotel. I was to be dressed in my Air Force Blues while Kathy in a rented white gown. The plan after the wedding reception was to go to Niagara Falls. Our car was clean as a whistle. It had a "Just Married" soap signs in the windows and old shoes dragging behind on ropes. We planned to drive back to Eglin in the Ford, and we eventually did. Well, the car was not cooperative because as soon as we got on the New York State Thruway, the red light for the alternator came on. I stopped at a gas station on the thruway and the attendant said that he would see if they could install new brushes for the alternator. They did successfully repair the generator.

That evening, we arrived at Niagara Falls. We did the touristy things one does at the falls, which can be very little. The majesty of the falls was muted because repairs were being done at the American Falls. The Maid of the Mist boat was closer to the Canadian Falls. It was full of tourists that did not mind getting wet from the mist. We didn't stay long, and the next day, we made plans to go back to Williamstown and to start our trip to Eglin AFB.

In 1961, regular gasoline was selling for about $0.259 in Massachusetts. Connecticut had a gas war going on, and the selling price was $0.12. On the way down to Florida, our car got pretty good mileage at about twenty-five miles to the gallon. We kept seeing gas signs with $0.12 cents on them. Curiosity got the best of us. We stopped and found out that that was before tax. We still needed gas on the way down, so we bought anyway. We took short naps in rest areas, and before we knew it, we were nearly at Eglin. We came to the town of Crestview, about twenty-five miles north of Eglin. When I had first come to Eglin, I had looked into the possibilities of renting in Crestview. I stopped at the Air Force Social Club in Crestview that catered to Eglin personnel and asked around. They had made some suggestions, so Kathy and I drove around the town. We found a small two-bedroom apartment on a side road just south of the railroad tracks with a rental sign hung on the door. We inquired with the neighbors, and they told us who the owner was and where he lived. So we went to his home and inquired about the rent. When he said $45 a month, with a first month's rent in advance, we said yes right away! Our landlord gave us the key to the front door as we left. We had arrived!

The next step was to get propane into the tank behind the building. Our apartment used it for heat (with portable heaters) and also the stove in the kitchen. Crestview was three hundred feet above sea level. The weather was still damp and chilly even if it was in Florida. Then we went grocery shopping at the base PX. We needed food and cleaning materials. The bed in the bedroom required some sheets, pillows, and covers. Coffee and hamburgers were to be our first delicacies at the apartment. We went to the administrative building and logged in. I brought the car over for inspection so that we could go freely through the gate at Valparaiso. I was surprised that the headlights would get so much attention. The lamps had to use a yellow cast bulb no larger than thirty-five watts and adjustments for how high the law permitted. The brakes, windows, muffler system, and struts came through okay. We decided that was enough for the first day.

In the morning, we had breakfast and then made friends with the neighbors. Everyone was friendly and we made friends easily. The staff sergeant next door was glad that I was going to be stationed at the main base. He needed another rider to fill his four-door Chevrolet Corvair for the thirty-mile trip to Eglin. The interesting thing about this car was that the engine was in the back. He had two sergeants who were already riding with him. I arranged to use our Ford as another vehicle for the four of us. We each chose a day to drive and it worked out okay.

In the morning, I went to the base with my new friends and left the car for Kathy to use for anything she had to do that day. When I got home, I found Kathy and our neighbor's wife in the kitchen putting bandages on Kathy's lower legs. Thank goodness the burns did not seem too extreme and Kathy just shooed it off. She explained that she had never used a gas oven before. She had set a meat loaf as our first night's meal. When she went to light the burner on the oven, the match she had flamed out before she could get the oven lit. She scrounged for about two minutes for another matchstick. Kathy did not realize the danger she was in. When she struck the match to light the oven, the released gas exploded. Thank goodness she wasn't hurt badly! Lesson learned.

That was only one of the interesting things we learned about our apartment. In the morning, it was still dark when we got up and lit the kitchen light. It was a familiar sight to me because as a child, we had a similar situation in our apartment on Miller Street in Adams, Massachusetts. The walls and ceiling were covered with cockroaches, probably at least a couple of hundreds! I immediately went to our landlord, and he gave me a sprayer with about a gallon of roach spray in it. I used it to kill off the majority of the roaches.

The neighbors across from our apartment had large bunches of bamboo with kittens that had just been born and hiding in that shrubbery. I saw the kittens and caught one of the kittens and put it in a box as a surprise to Kathy. When she opened the box, with her gift inside, the kitten jumped out and hid under our couch. With a little coaching by some milk in a small bowl, he became very friendly and began purring. That cat must have lived nine lives, as they say about cats, because after two months of growth, he went out our front door when someone opened it. He was hit at the neckline by the spring-loaded door. He was knocked out and I was preparing to put him in a small box and bury him in our backyard. All of a sudden, he started meowing again and I brought him back into the apartment. After another month, the kitten developed a white ring, about 1.5 inches in diameter (like a halo), around his neck on the spot where he had been hit by the door. He had a good appetite after that, and he would jump up the back of our couch all the way to the ceiling to eat the huge Janitor (some people called them Jupiter bugs) for breakfast and lunch. Florida did have a lot of bugs!

*****

Before Kathy and I went to Niagara Falls, Earl had found us a 1947 Ford sedan that had rust on the body panels, but the car seemed to run good. Eventually we had to leave for Eglin AFB and get settled in at our apartment in Crestview. The car did get us to Crestview, Florida, when my leave was up. I did my best to patch them with rags and it at least kept the air flow down to a reasonable delay. Florida weather was warm in the spring and summer, but later in the year, the patches would hardly get by. I would have to consider purchasing another vehicle and increase my income by fall. The members of our carpool were already complaining about the air noise and drafts.

It was job hunting I would go! I knew that I had some talents when it came to working in a garage just prior to my military training. Pumping gas and fixing flats at service station would help. I had also heard that the local softball league needed an umpire. I knew about umpiring from my younger years in Massachusetts. The teams played two games a day on Saturday and Sunday at the local baseball field and paid $8 per day. The following spring, I took on a Little League team. Although there was no money, it was good experience.

I checked Bullock's TV repair shop in Crestview. Mr. Bullock said, "I'm always looking for good help! I've been working on this TV on the bench behind me. Here, use this multimeter. Check it out." A master sergeant on base had given me a chassis for a fourteen-inch black-and-white TV. He had a schematic from the base library and had already scrounged available parts the US Air Force had given him. This gave me a heads up as to how to use the meter to measure voltages and shorts in the unit that Mr. Bullock was working on. I pointed out that the capacitor had failed. He said, "Let's see if you are right." He reached in, clipped the old capacitor from both ends, and soldered the leads of the good capacitor to the tube socket that I had been working on. I was right because the tube fired up properly when Mr. Bullock turned the set on. He suggested replacing the old tube to ensure the life of the set chassis. He had outfoxed me into how much faster his way was. Mr. Bullock hired me for part-time work!

My Neighbor and His New Four-Door Corvair Sedan

John, the staff sergeant and also my next-door neighbor who was in our carpool, was the driver for the next time the group would be driving to work at Eglin AFB. I sat in the right front passenger seat. The others in our car pool were much heavier than John or me, so they sat in the back seat. We left Crestview at seven o'clock that morning for Eglin.

John had serviced his car himself and had pumped thirty-two pounds of air into the front and rear tires. He had done that out of habit, as he had in all his previous cars. The speed limit heading toward Eglin was sixty-five miles per hour. When the car reached the posted speed limit, the tires on the front of the car rose off the ground. The steering wheel was turning free! Pure momentum had kept us going straight. John learned quickly to slow the car down. He was visibly shaken, as were his passengers! I asked John how much air was in the tires and he told us thirty-two pounds. It was obvious that the tires were overinflated. The tires were supposed to be set to twelve pounds of air pressure. We stopped and lowered the tire pressure as soon as we could.

*****

My daughter Trina was born in the base hospital on July 21, 1961. My wife Kathy had been visiting one of the base doctors on routine follow-up checkups. They told her that Trina could be expected soon and that Kathy should stay at the base on the morning of July 20th just in case.

They sent me back to work in the Electronics Building. I was working that early that morning on a radio set that needed calibration when the telephone rang for me to come to the hospital. The nurse, who had made the call, said, "Congratulations on the birth of your daughter Trina. Come this afternoon and be ready to transport your wife Kathy and the baby home!" We had a bassinet, a crib, and clothes for the baby at the apartment. Trina looked really cute wearing her bonnet, a small white dress, and booties. That afternoon, we went immediately home to our apartment in Crestview.

We had a surprise visit from Earl and Lucille Estes. Earl had purchased a 1955 Citroen automobile. This car was strange looking by any standard. It had the appearance of a flying saucer! The car was built in France and had a hydraulic lever control that adjusted the chassis both up and down for better ride comfort (no springs). The French presidents use these cars as their limousine. Earl really liked this car and drove it on the trip from Massachusetts to Crestview, Florida. A railroad track crossed over Main Street just before entering Crestview. The highway dipped up and down over these tracks. Earl took us for a ride and drove rather fast over that dip. He had released his hydraulic lever control to maximum height to demonstrate a smooth ride over the track. It was indeed an eye-opener.

After Earl's demo, we went back to our apartment and along with John and his wife, our neighbors, proceeded to barbecue a huge steak. It just barely fit on the barbecue. We had a delicious meal. The steak was tender and delicious. Beer helped to wet the whistle.

I had built and painted (white) a multidrawer dresser to hold all the clothing and presents that Trina had received from relatives and friends. Trina was still dressed in white and Kathy placed her other clothes and baby blankets in appropriate drawers in the dresser.

Having met the new baby, Lucille and Earl headed for home as they had a business to run. Our dog, not wanting to be left out in the picture, had a litter of puppies on the way, and along with the kittens from the bushes next door, we had a full house.

The next month, Jessie, my mother, and my sister Mary came to see us and the baby. They flew in from Bradley Field in Massachusetts to Memphis, Tennessee. They boarded a C-54 commercial flight to Eglin AFB and landed at the civilian facilities there. I picked them up and brought them to our apartment.

We were glad to see them and of course they were also glad to see Trina. The following day, we headed for the white-sand beaches at Fort Walton Beach, with the clear water and beautiful sunshine. I had taken some vacation time to appreciate our time together. That way, we could enjoy our activities.

We spent the day at the beach and thoroughly enjoyed the day. Even the dog loved the swimming, as she kept chasing a stick that everyone kept throwing into the water.

For this occasion, I had purchased a black-and-white 1955 Chevrolet Bel Air sedan. We all appreciated this car. I had it all polished up and it was clean as a whistle. I knew that my carpool would also appreciate this car over the old Ford when we go to work on Monday (no more drafty rear panels).

We discussed going to the Space Center at Cape Canaveral on the east side of Florida. It was about a three-hour trip. There we visited the museum for the Apollo space activities and were shown the Saturn rockets, large movers for the spacecraft, launch facilities, and space memorabilia. We saw the inside of the data center and had a briefing on the itinerary of the upcoming missions from the controllers. We had just missed any of the actual launches that were heading for the moon. When I returned to Eglin, I was able to hear the actual launches on our radio gear. Mom and Mary left for home after two more days in Crestview and Eglin AFB flight lines with all of our aircraft visible for viewing. They left from Eglin and proceeded to Bradley Field in Connecticut without any glitches.

Recreational Activities

I had twelve months left in my career in the US Air Force and would be unemployed by the end of 1962. I decided to concentrate on activities that would interest me. Those activities included repairing television, being a Little League coach, and playing for the US Air Force baseball team in Alabama, Northern Florida, and Georgia. The Little League team I coached won their league that year.

The US Air Force team was a different matter. We played in cow pastures for the league, and I was made a pitcher for that team with very little success. I never could throw a curveball. I took the signs from the catcher but I always pitched a fastball with minimum curves. I could hit a long ball though! The one thing interesting about being on the US Air Force team was when we went to Alabama. Our driver had just recently purchased four recap tires for his car. When we were approaching Alabama, all four recaps fell off and our driver had to replace them all.

Ready to Go Home from the US Air Force

The Little League had a wagon used as a concession stand and built as a Conestoga-style wagon but with two sixteen-inch tires instead of wheels. They said that they would be willing to sell it to me at a reasonable price. I thought about it and said that I would be interested at the end of their season.

I decided to make an offer, because I needed to plan to carry all of our possessions all the way to Massachusetts. We agreed to a relatively low price of $200. I attached a hitch and drove it to the apartment.

September came around rather quickly, and I made preparations to load the wagon with all of our belongings. I had even traded a spaghetti dinner to one of the sergeant, who worked in the warehouse. He said, "Do not turn my tools in to the supply depot. I will take care of the paperwork." I needed those tools when we had to replace the tires on the way home.

I loaded the wagon with ultimate care. I did not want too much weight on the tongue of the hitch in either direction. We made preparations to depart. The best of luck does not always come my way.

We went straight north on Route 11 toward the Florida line. Driving with care, I thought that everything would be fine. I did not feel any problems with the trailer. The roads of yesteryear were not always in the best of condition.

Unfortunately, one of the tires blew out and I now had to replace the sixteen-inch tires. I left Kathy to watch the wagon. Finding sixteen-inch tires seemed like an unlikely effort. I came upon a filling station that had two sixteen-inch tires in stock! I had to pull the old tires off the wagon and set the axles down on the roadway with the jack. Using the same jack, I raised the axle for each tire and mounted each tire. After tightening the lug bolts, we were ready to roll. I called the station and asked them to collect the tires, and I would leave the employee a few dollars inside one of the tires.

This had taken about two hours total, and we had lost that time to get underway.

CHAPTER 15

My Various Jobs at GE and IBM

We purchased an older home in Dalton, Massachusetts, for $300 with a small mortgage. We located this home in the local want ads. The lawyer for the previous owner was glad to handle the sale and he assisted in the mortgage.

Dalton is a small town just off Route 8 and Route 9 near Pittsfield. Dalton's claim to fame was to support General Electric (GE) with employees and provided print shop, just down the road from us, to print all the US paper bills for the entire nation. They unfortunately did not have a job for me at their establishment.

In the back of the house was a grassy lot with a ten by twelve work shed with work benches and AC power. It would be the perfect place for me to do my television. The previous owner had moved on and left the house in the care of his lawyer. The house was a three-bedroom ranch on a cement slab. It had a natural gas furnace, a kitchen, a small living room, and some storage closets throughout the rest of the house. We brought as much of our furniture as we could from the shed at the Willows Motel in Williamstown, Massachusetts. This was all of our belongings that we had brought from Eglin AFB in Florida.

For the kitchen, my cousin Hank brought us some chairs and a table loaned from St. Thomas Church in Adams, where he was employed as a janitor. The heat in the house was inadequate because the cement slab that the house sat on had shifted upward about three inches from being level by the frost and ice formation along the driveway. During the cold months, we had to stuff newspaper in the cracks around the kitchen floor area to be able to sit at the table. This problem needed to be fixed! I had little extra money to support major repairs, so I had to improvise. The driveway was gravel based and that would make it easier for me to jury-rig a repair job. What I had in mind was to dig a coffinlike hole outside and along the kitchen wall. It ended up to be about 3.5 feet wide to about twelve feet in length and 2.5 feet deep. I was able to lift the edge of the slab about three inches by using my car's jack. I purchased peastone in plastic bags and fiberglass insulation rolls with sufficient amounts to fill the "casket." I also pushed some of both the stone and fiberglass insulation into the gap below the slab. I completed the task over the weekend, and it worked like a charm! I felt a little sorry for the previous owner.

I was working inside my television repair shop with a customer's television when Kathy came out and rather excitingly called out to me, "JFK has been shot!" It was hard to believe. I quickly turned up the volume and listened to the broadcast of the horrific news. We both felt horrible about the situation.

We were anxious to improve our income and we were anxious to sell. We had little else or reason to go anywhere, so what could we do?

We worked the want ads. The hotel ad we found on the *Berkshire Eagle* newspaper about a motel manager/owner of the Yankee Inn Motel on Route 7 in Lenox, Massachusetts, looking for someone familiar with motel operations seemed like right down our alley. We discussed the job and he asked us to come over for the interview. The job was for three months or until the season was over for the tourists. The clincher was the experience with the Willows Motel in Williamstown. We were satisfied with the salary and accommodations and the timing. We got the job!

The next ad we had to pursue was the three-month rental for the GE people. They were having problems getting a place for such a dedicated time, but it all worked out in the end. They agreed to the price of $300 for three months. It actually was two weeks longer. We were in luck.

Selling was next on the agenda for our home in Dalton. We now had a three-month period to sell with a good chance of pulling that off. We discussed with the lawyer the possibility of still going bankrupt, but he was not interested. He said that he would work on the sale and eventually that also went our way.

When we arrived at our motel, the manager asked us to take over the pool maintenance as a slightly added workload. This was okay with us. Apparently it was okay with our daughter Trina, because she walked right off the back wall of the pool into the deep water. Kathy nearly panicked and fully dressed jumped into the pool and took hold of Trina. In just a few moments, the danger was over.

We were able to send quite a few customers to the Willows Motel as they did not have as much traffic as the Yankee Motel. Earl and Lucille had their full sign on almost every weekend, sometimes for three or four days. Earl said that he was getting calls from the hotels nearby asking him what his secret was! (We kept the Yankee Inn Motel vacancy sign lit to encourage the tourists to inquire.) The Yankee Inn was also full during those times, and our manager gave us a bonus for several months. Everybody was happy.

The first job I had at GE was in the Navy's Polaris guidance lab near the GE High Voltage plant at Merrill Road in Pittsfield. The lab was to be shut down in a month or so after I started. I was laid off from the plant and was able to get a job as a technician in the instrumentation lab in the GE High Voltage Lab facility just down the road.

A couple of weeks went by and a couple of Navy recruiters came to the lab. They were there to recruit technicians for an opportunity to get a US Navy job on one of the newest atomic submarines, the USS Thresher (SSN-593). They were very good at their job, but I get very sick on the sea, and being confined underwater was not my cup of tea. I turned them down.

On the USS Thresher's debut, 220 miles east of Cape Cod, at a depth of 8,400 feet in the Atlantic Ocean, the Thresher exploded with all hands lost. Sometimes the risk is not worth it!

I worked as a calibration technician on the various test instrumentation for a manager named Bob Leonard. Most of the equipment was simple power supplies and digital voltage meters. Many of the instruments were made by Hewlett-Packard and an offshoot company called Dymec. During the next couple of months, I was being bumped by an engineer who was being let go from the manufacturing line and he appealed to management that union employees were to get first dibs on any available position. With that, I was about to be let go. Bob Leonard, my boss, felt sorry for me and said that he had met another manager who was in the process of setting up a calibration lab in New York at the East Fishkill and Poughkeepsie plants for IBM's new computer systems. He said that his name was Ed Leonard and he would give him a call to see if he was interested in me for an interview. He made the call and gave me directions to go south on the Taconic Parkway and west on Route 55. I was to stop at the IBM office there on Monday morning and announce who I was and my intent.

I was off and running. Well, running is probably a word that sometimes plays tricks on you. As instructed, I went from Pittsfield to Route 20 and then south to the Taconic Parkway. At that time, the parkway ended at half the distance than today. So I followed instructions and went south to Route 55. When I came to Route 55, I turned west, and lo and behold just a short distance from the Taconic, I came upon a building with the words IBM on it. Oh well, nothing ventured, nothing gained. It was a small office building that seemed to be the IBM that I was looking for. I was not impressed, as I had envisioned a large facility. I went to the receptionist and asked for Ed Leonard. Jack Tilghman can fill in for Mr. Leonard. There were many instruments that need calibration. The Hewlett-Packard Company manufactured instruments under the HP nameplate, but it also did so with a different brand name, Dymec. The ones I was familiar with were small meters that were relatively easy to calibrate. When I was interviewed by Jack Tilghman, he asked what type of instrumentation I worked on. I told him that one brand of instrument that I was used to working on was the Dymec meters. He immediately picked up on that one and said that he was glad to hear that I had the experience in Dymec equipment. At this point, Jack said that I was a good candidate and he offered me a position in the calibration lab in Fishkill at a salary of $115. I had hoped for more, but I could tell that he had the best offer he could make. I said that I'd have to think about it. So I ended up leaving without an official yes, because it would have been hard to go through the relocation to the Fishkill–Poughkeepsie area.

That effectively ended the interview. I was shown where the much larger IBM facility was on Route 9. Now I was impressed.

I went back home without a solid position. I took a few days to look into other potential job offerings in Massachusetts. I spent another week in the television shop in North Adams where I had been doing antenna installations. By the end of that time, an IBM recruiter called and asked why I had not accepted the position. He said that the position at $105 was a good offer. I told him that I had been offered $115. I asked, "What is going on?" The recruiter said that he would get back to me. He almost immediately called back and said that I would qualify for IBM to supply the transport of our home goods at their costs and they would raise the offer back to the $115. I accepted. It took me two years to get my first raise!

The next step for us was to find a home in the Hopewell Junction area. We saw a for sale sign on the office just down the street on Elk Road. We settled on the purchase of our home in Worley Homes development when we came to an agreement with the developer, Tex Worley, who said that the house was priced at $14,200. I asked if he would consider a rental offer. He said, "No, but I will sell you the house." I was hesitant because I did not have sufficient funds to come up with the down payment. Tex Worley offered that he would give us the down payment of $4,200. He would expect monthly payments, but I would have to apply for a bank mortgage. The first payment of Tex's agreement was signed on my personal check with a notation that included the cash requirement and we agreed to a repayment schedule. The mortgage of $10,000 was handled by a local bank. The down payment that we had agreed to with Tex Worley was completed by the end of two years. I even sold a new television to Tex and his wife at a cost of $250 that I used as part of the agreement for the down payment. We moved into our home that month.

IBM, as agreed, paid for the movement of our furniture and personal items from Massachusetts to Hopewell Junction. I took the first month or so putting AC power, hot water, heat, a work bench for my TV work, a six-foot bar for the family room, sheetrock for the ceiling, and pine paneling in the lower level of our raised ranch home. This was to be our partying room.

I met Mike and Carmen Diaz and they had two children and a dog. Mike and I hit it off well and we discussed the hunting in the area. We both decided to join the Whortlekill Rod and Gun Club in Hopewell Junction and proceeded to utilize the many acres of land they had on lease. The club also had a large lake in the rear of the clubs property that was stocked with trout.

Our other two nearest neighbors were friendly. They both had many children, one with twelve kids and the other with eleven children. They were members of the Catholic Church in Hopewell Junction and were very good Catholics.

When I got the job at IBM, Jack Tilghman, my new manager, had his lead technician show me the Dymec test equipment. I was introduced to the technician who brought me into a large room with a highly sophisticated measurement device that was capable of measurements in the GHz range and beyond. This equipment was well beyond my ability to handle at this point. Jack agreed to help out.

Our lead technician was asked to contact various vendors that we had continuous involvement with, and he scheduled technical demonstrations and brief classes on the more sophisticated instrumentation. These included the Dymec testers, electron microscopes, optical microscopes, oscilloscopes, digital voltmeters, and chemical test equipment. The chemical manager was very helpful in my learning his needs of his more sophisticated instruments and that I should be the key technician to oversee those needs.

This was the start of my long-term commitment to IBM and our new home. Trina, our first daughter, was now close to getting a new sister. Kathy was nine months pregnant and had already chosen the name. The baby was going to be named Sue Ann.

At the time, our family car was a 1991 Ford station wagon. It was dark blue and had seen better days, but I thought we could go a little longer with it. We still used it for our trips to Massachusetts to visit with our families. Little did we know that problems would start soon.

When going up and down Taconic Parkway, the car's engine would spit, sputter, lose power, and then straighten out and run smoothly again. I decided that I had better investigate the cause. I took the air cleaner off the engine and looked down the throat of the carburetor. There was nothing drastically wrong with the carburetor. It was the air filter that had a problem. At first glance into the air cleaner, the air filter looked like it was brand new. But the surrounding sides of the air filter had a perfectly installed ring of straw inside. I reached in and started pulling the straw out. I realized that one of the chipmunks that lived in our garage had packed the air filter with straw to make a nest for his or her family. The straw would break off into small pieces because of the air pressure going through the spout of the air cleaner and into the carburetor. I pulled it all out and reinstalled the air filter within the air cleaner. I put the air cleaner back in place, and the engine ran smoothly for quite a while.

The alternator was the next thing to go. Then the electric wires caught fire under the hood and filled the garage with smoke. I was able to get new wiring to repair that. It was time to consider a newer car.

I remembered that there was a small car dealer in on Route 82 in Hopewell Junction. I felt that the small dealer might be easier to negotiate with than the sprawling large dealers on Route 9, with huge lots filled with cars. I had no intention of spending lots of money, and I had a used car in mind. I approached the dealer and saw that he indeed had some nice cars on his front line, but I never dreamt that he would have a 1964 Mustang available.

Ford had just started delivering Mustangs to their dealers and somehow they had one in Hopewell ahead of the Ford dealer in Poughkeepsie. The dealer in Poughkeepsie had pulled a large sheet off the car he was hoping to sell me when they had their celebration demo the next weekend. He had just shown me a 1974 Ford Falcon and whispered, "I shouldn't be showing this yet." I was not interested.

The Mustang was such a beautiful car to me that I wanted it the moment I saw it at the Hopewell dealership. It was a two-door coupe and had a six-cylinder four-speed shift with a 101-horsepower engine. I said, "You give me your best price and I will consider whether or not to buy it right now. There are a lot of Ford dealers around the area." His price was $300 down, with a balance of $2,800 plus tax, and I said yes. I financed it through our credit union that same day. I couldn't wait to show the car to Kathy. Kathy was delighted with the car.

The very next week, Kathy gave birth to Sue Ann Shafer. The hospital kept Kathy for only two days. Sue was our second child. Kathy couldn't wait for a third. She had already picked out a name for a third girl (she was sure she would have another girl) and the name was Kathleen. I was given my instructions as to what Kathy needed for the baby's first ride in our brand new mustang.

Continued IBM Management Support

The education department at IBM was a change that was interesting to me. Every month, we would watch a war movie to develop decision-making skills of our managers. While enjoying the movie, managers were expected to learn how the officers in army made everyday decisions that were crucial to the war effort during World War II. Many of the decision-makers in the army had no knowledge of the end results when they sent men and machines on crucial missions from which the bombers and airmen would not return. When the bombers were to be sent, the officers would decide how many bombers were needed. Many planes never returned.

Our managers decided to have Engineering produce chips based on database measurements that would support our products' integrity. We built the first of single chips on a square one-inch wafer that had to produce as expected. Many of those chips were on priority needs for our customers. These chips were in the computers for the space rockets heading for the moon. There was no room for error. Chip production rapidly expanded with substantial chip count.

We received the first eight IBM Personal Computers with two disk drives. These drives had only 10 MB of data available and were delivered to our classrooms for immediate use. We were in a race against several computer makers. We had to get our people up to speed with the first software products available to our engineers. I was involved in setting up classes for programs like Basic and VisiCalc, the first engineering space sheet, later to become Excel.

The next adventure for me was the installation of a 4341 VM computer with my programmers and engineers to be able to converse with France and other facilities like Burlington, Vermont. At the time this was in place, I managed eight programmers and thirty engineers supporting our efforts.

John Akers from Corporate Headquarters came to my twenty-fifth anniversary with IBM, and I was given a Rolex watch and a special management citation for my efforts.

A downsizing was inevitable at East Fishkill shortly after, and I retired from IBM on my twenty-ninth year, but in that same year, I was given a thirtieth year as a free pass with continued financial support for that year.

After my retirement, I spent the next five years at the Vassar College Golf Course as a manager of the Pro Shop. This was followed by Driver Education for ten years, driving students on both the road and classroom training. Selling cars were next, followed by several years in real estate.

ROBERT SHAFER

John F. Akers
Old Orchard Road, Armonk, New York 10504-1783

March 23, 1989

Dear Bob,

On this special occasion, I would like to add my personal thanks for your twenty-five years of dedicated service to IBM.

Your enthusiasm and innovation over the years have contributed greatly to the success of our company. In addition, I now look to your wisdom and judgment to guide us in the days ahead.

You have my best wishes for continued success in the future.

Sincerely,

John

Mr. Robert S. Shafer Jr.
IBM Corporation
East Fishkill
Hopewell Junction, NY 12533

CHAPTER 16

Early Fishing Experiences

F irst and foremost, get a fishing license before fishing any stream or lake in New York! For New York state residents, a fee of $25 is charged for sixteen to seventy years old and $5 for residents over seventy years old. The license is good for one year from the date of purchase. Out-of-state fees cost $50. There are several other categories. Check with the Department of Environmental Conservation (DEC) website since most fees vary by the actual fishery area you might be fishing in.

*****

Whaley Lake is located 3.1 miles from Pawling off New York Route 292. The best fishing times for Whaley Lake are around 12:34 a.m. to 2:43 a.m. and 1:04 p.m. to 3:04 p.m. But first, you need to get the proper equipment for the type of fishing you are going to do. Tip-ups for ice fishing, use live bait. Use a six- to eight-pound test line (monofilament is fine) with your rod and reel combo. This could also be used as one of your tip-up holes if you chose to just hang out near your favorite hole. You can also use your trout fishing rod combo from your boat or the shore. Don't forget sunglasses to reduce glare.

Large Mouth Bass

Bass at Whaley Lake weigh in at an average of two to four pounds. All bass caught out of the regular season for bass must be returned unharmed to the lake. Bass fishing seasons starts on the third Saturday of June and lasts until November 30. There is a limit of five bass per day, twelve inches in size or larger per angler.

Bass are prevalent throughout the lake and small pond areas where you can find open areas near the lily pads across the railroad tracks. They tend to hide near shores that are protected by foliage and prefer the shallower waters. Bass are top feeders in general and will strike top surface poppers and other lures with lust! Just cast your line to an appropriate place. A good trick is to cast your line just over a small limb with the lure hanging just above the waterline. Let the lure slide down to the surface and cause ripples by bouncing it off the water. If any bass worth its salt spots this happening, he will strike with glee! In shallow areas, retrieve your lure slowly and stop occasionally. Wait a short time and continue reeling. Wait again and continue. Your bass may follow the lure all the way to your boat! There are sufficient days of summer to enjoy fishing for bass at Whaley Lake without having to go any real distances.

Good luck!

Yellow Perch

Different species of perch are prevalent in many large lakes and many countries around the world. They can weigh a great deal more than those at Whaley Lake. They are respected as excellent fish for eating at many fine restaurants. Yellow perch at Whaley Lake weigh in at approximately one to four pounds and usually are panfried after slicing the meat from the body of the fish.

When fishing for perch during the ice season, tip-ups or rod and reel could be used one hole at a time.

Perch tend to be smaller than bass and prefer minnows and insect larvae as bait. They will also strike plastic look-alikes. With your standard rod and reel outfit, you can double up using your trout poles and lures with the same basics that apply to trout fishing. You can catch a lot of perch and should use common sense as to how many you need.

Bluegill and Other Similar Species

Bluegills and other small similar species are present at Whaley Lake and weigh in at a quarter of a pound to less than one pound. They can be eaten and panfried with butter after slicing the meat off the bone. It probably would be okay if you had no other species of fish to eat. I personally might decide to use this fish as plant or fertilizer in the garden food!

Bluegills tend to gather in and around docks, boulders, and other shallow waters. Fly fishing with streamers tend to be popular ways of catching them. A bobber is a great way to teach and relax. Buy your child a small fishing pole since a longer rod might be too long for the child to handle. I will bet the proprietor of the bait shop would agree. I am sure he would have an excellent rod for your youngster. Your children would surely enjoy the excitement of catching a bluegill with their new rod while learning about fishing.

Best bets are live bait (one- or two-inch minnows), fishworm, night crawlers, crickets, or grasshoppers. Set your hook gently and return any small fish to the lake quickly so they don't die.

Grass Pickerel

Whaley Lake has grass pickerel, the smallest fish in the pike family. They seldom exceed ten to twelve inches in length. They are quite bony, and unless you really enjoy eating bones, I would not try to use them for lunch. They are very aggressive with a mouthful of teeth. Catching one can give you quite a fight.

Information, as in the above, is available online using Cortana for Windows desktops and laptops.

CHAPTER 17

Short Stories that Happened in 1964 and 1965

Winter: Whaley Lake Ice Fishing

During the December 1964 holidays, my wife and I and our children visited with my parents in Adams, Massachusetts. During this visit, I talked to my brothers and dad about the ice fishing they had planned or had already done at Cheshire Lake in Cheshire and Windsor Lake in Savoy. It's a lot colder there than in Dutchess County, New York, where we lived. I asked if there was any ice fishing gear that I could take home with me. I knew that they would be generous and offer any extras. I had used quite a bit of the ice fishing equipment in my last fishing experience with them and actually some were truly my own anyway.

My brother John and I went out to the work shed at the farm and selected ten wooden tip-ups (these tip-ups were the best available at the time), a five-foot ice pick, a bait pail, and a box that could hold them. We made a sled out of the box and attached a rope to pull it. We needed to attach two planks on the bottom to act as ski and a board across the front that was at a forty-five-degree angle that would allow it to glide on the ice and to plow through any snow. A second board would be needed to be placed on the forty-five-degree board. Some master carpentry would be needed here. Nothing to it!

The tip-ups were complete with a reel, twenty feet of fish line, and an appropriate-size hook and folded neatly. Each fisherman was to be limited to five tip-ups. We would have to make an eight-inch hole in the ice with the ice pick. That size might not be large enough in lakes where northern pike were present, but I am not aware of any of these species being in Whaley Lake. I did not believe our eight-inch hole needed to be enlarged as long as we were fishing at Whaley Lake. We just had to be careful in handling the ice pick and not lose it into the lake. To avoid that possibility, we needed to drill a hole in the handle and use a long leather shoestring and tie it around our wrist. A gasoline-powered auger would have been great but one can't be greedy! The bait pail would hold plenty of bait. We returned home to Hopewell Junction via the Taconic Parkway, which at that time had not yet been connected to the Massachusetts thruway. The trip took about two hours.

Mike and I and our wives met for coffee at his house at Deer Lane. We discussed all the exciting adventures we knew about in fishing in Whaley Lake near Pawling, off Route 292. Locals had suggested we start there. We wanted to take advantage of the winter months as much as possible. Few lakes and ponds had any better fishing than Whaley Lake. Mike previously lived in New York City and had little or no experience either fishing or hunting. Sportsman's magazines helped but there is nothing like the real thing. I had previous experience in both hunting and fishing, as I had recently came from a farm family in the Berkshires of Massachusetts, where these activities were the norm.

The winter months were well under way, and January would be the best time to go ice fishing. When I lived on the farm, I had fished through the ice at Hoosic River in Cheshire, Massachusetts, with my family, many times. Based on my previous experience and the equipment I had brought home, it would take little effort and money to get started and needs would be minimal. We decided that we would go to Whaley Lake, which is local, and scout the area. For safety's sake, one thing we needed to know was how thick the ice was. We could observe if other fishermen were already fishing out there on the ice. We would be dressed in our hunting clothes, wearing leather hunting boots, and our hunting hats. In really cold weather, we might have to include long johns under the hunting shirt and pants. If the wind was blowing across the ice, it could get pretty cold. A small fire would have to be built to avoid frostbite.

Our visit to Whaley Lake was very informative. We talked to the proprietor at the lake's bait shop and he gave us some good information. The lake was in jeopardy. The dam at the south end of the lake was falling apart and the town was trying to get the lake stable. The overflow showed about one-foot lower than you would expect. The lake would have slightly lower water levels until it was fixed. By spring, the water should be higher when the overflow repairs are completed. There was no immediate danger. He told us that the bait cost $0.10 per bait fish. He sold $1 hot dogs and $0.50 chocolate ice popsicles on weekends. There was a $2 charge to access the lake at his boat launching facilities in the spring and summer. He said that he would not charge us to access the lake until April 1st. The lake is quite large at about 3.7 square miles of water. The distance across was about five hundred feet wide. The lake in the spring and fall months could handle fairly large speedboats. There were two ponds across from the railroad track filled with lily pads, which are excellent for bass fishing. Each pond was approximately twenty acres each of fishable water. There were half a dozen ice fishermen on the lake and they were catching a lot of yellow perch and bluegills. We told him that we would be back next weekend. We thanked him for the invite and information and headed home.

By the next weekend, we had completed fixing up our bait box and checking out our gear, clothing, socks, hats, gloves, matches, boots, and license. We were ready to go. It had snowed a couple of inches, and the temperature was in the midtwenties with some minor wind coming out of the north. Mid-January was calling! It would be pretty cold.

We dressed at home with our cold weather gear and we left at about 7:00 a.m. and arrived at the bait shop at about eight o'clock. I had driven my Ford station wagon to be able to carry all the gear and the two of us. Mike had brought a couple of miniature ginger brandies and coffee, just enough to ensure a little taste to offset the cold. Hot cocoa was the next best thing, and I brought a thermos of hot chocolate for warmth and peanut butter sandwiches to satisfy our bellies.

When we got to the lake, we purchased twenty bait fish from the bait shop, a $2 investment. It was a good thing he opened at 8:00 a.m. We unloaded our gear and equipment and proceeded to the dock area. We tested the ice for safety and proceeded toward the islands near the railroad track side of the lake. The lake was kind of scary as the ice kept talking with the cracking sound you could hardly get used to. The next thing we did was to search for firewood to build a fire on the nearest island and started a fire to warm us as we needed it. No, we did not use the old Indian way. We used matches!

With our ice pick, we started poking holes in the ice to give us access to the lake water. The exercise kept us warm, and we soon had five holes chipped clear. We skimmed the ice out with the skimming tool I had bought during the week. We started to set up our tip-ups and get something going before we finished cutting more holes. We attached the minnows with the single hook just behind the dorsal fin. We fed our line until we knew that we had the bait to five or six feet deep into the water. We slipped the metal strap, which is designed to slide to the top (approximately twelve inches), above the upright tip-up when standing in the hole in the ice. There is a metal bar from the reel to the bottom of the flag strap. That bar release also controlled the reel motion indictor. The release metal rod and clip allowed the red flag to wave into the air twelve inches above the wooden tip-up. If a fish pulled the line from the reel, which is at the bottom of the tip-up, it turns one full revolution, and then that turn would cause the release. Once released by the clips, the flag swings into the air and the continued turning of the reel would cause the flag to wave. Once we see the flag waving, we had a good possibility of a "fish on the hook" moving with the bait. Then we'd have to follow through on the actual catch of the fish.

We observed the tracks and ponds on the west side of the tracks and glanced at the other small islands nearby and added wood to the fire to ensure that we had heat. We took a close look for other fishermen's access holes that they had chopped the previous day to see if we could get the remaining five holes that we still needed to fill our limit of ten tip-ups. It would be easier to chop thin ice that other fishermen had used on the previous day. We decided after finding several holes with only a little ice left in them. We completed the last five holes. After arming the flags on our tip-ups, we took a warm fire break. We sipped our coffee and cocoa. It never seems to amaze me how good that tasted when you are out on the ice! The warmth of the fire was exhilarating and lifted our spirits. We collected more wood from the island we were at. We put freshwater into the bucket that we had brought with us from home and patiently waited.

While we watched, we suddenly saw one of the tip-ups' flag flip up and wave in the air. This was a great moment. When we got to the flagged tip-up, we saw the line going out. Because the fish was moving, the turning reel caused the flag to wiggle. We envisioned a large fish on the other side of the line. Mike placed the tip-up onto the ice and grabbed the line. He carefully pulled the fish to the open hole. We had caught our first fish and it was only 9:00 a.m.! A large perch had taken the bait. It was about twelve inches long and weighed about two pounds. We put the fish in the bucket we had brought from home. Earlier we had filled it half full with water and ice, which would keep the fish fresh. We fished for several more hours and caught more perch than anything else. But we enjoyed the experience of being outdoors more than anything. On to our next trophy!

Spring and Summer: Development of Whortlekill Lake as a Gravel Pit

The Whortlekill Rod and Gun Club's Whortlekill Lake was registered with the New York State as a trout preserve. This allowed the club to regulate how many fish each member could catch. They were also allowed to fish for trout year-round. All fish caught had to be registered at the locked gateway to the facility.

After the first few years, the fishing committee decided to offer the public a chance to compete in big trout fishing tournaments, which became regular events and gave the club additional revenue to continue expanding the lake's income potential.

I spent twenty-five years on the board of directors and helped in many activities. There have been many experiences and friendships in the hunting, fishing, trapshooting, pistol range, and archery activities in the club. We went through years of growing pains, and I can only suggest that the club is now under better supervision now more than I can remember from the past.

We took two trips trout fishing in the month of April to the Catskill Mountains and the Adirondacks National Park, one trip to the Beaverkill River, and one to the Battenkill River. We spent quite a few outings trout fishing at the Whortlekill Rod and Gun Club's lake in Hopewell Junction. Mike and I had recently joined the club as members.

Whortlekill Lake Development/Fishing for Trout

Whortlekill Lake is a deepwater gravel pit that was dug down to the freshwater table. The club developed the lake to raise operating funds. The gravel dug from the lake was sold to local vendors. A large amount of the gravel was used to develop the then new IBM complex at East Fishkill, New York, which was a short distance from the club. The revenue from the gravel sales lowered membership costs, raised money to build raising ponds and buy feed and stock the lake with trout, build additional facilities for other activities, and lease and purchase game-related properties. The fishing would be free for members and family use. The club stocked several species of trout every year in the lake. There was a New York State requirement for registering the lake as a fishing preserve. The lake has a locked gate and a registration station for members to account for the fish they would catch.

Fishing in the spring time was with rods, reels, trout lures, and bait. In the winter months, tip-ups were used for fishing through the ice. The lake was continually developed since the depth and acreage were strictly controlled. Using a large construction tractor with a very tall cabled clamshell attachment, a depth of forty to sixty feet at the center areas of the pond was made, and this also provided grading to the shorelines. This gave us a good start to stock twelve- to fourteen-inch trout that were bought from local fish farms, each costing around $2. The number of purchased trout depended on the fishing committee's budget. The lake was more than a total of five acres at two hundred feet in width and more than 750 feet in length.

Some members wanted more fish, so the fishing committee developed a plan and proposed a budget to the board of directors. The plan was later expanded to have more fish by building two small ponds to raise about two thousand two- to three-inch trout. The ponds would have a shed and automated food feeders to ensure the baby trout would reach their maximum size. The plan was to use the depth of the lake to their advantage. We needed to provide electricity to pump the cold water. That water was twenty-five to twenty-eight degrees Fahrenheit as measured at the deeper depths, into the rearing ponds. Appropriate piping for plastic pipe and water pumps were also needed to transfer the water to the ponds. This was the start of great strides in length and numbers of fish available to the members. The first netting in the fall produced a thousand fifteen- to eighteen-inch rainbow and brook trout with weighing two to three pounds. There were still quite a few trout left in the pond, and we left them and fed them with our autofeeders to allow them to grow a little more before we harvested them. A second pond was being developed. Members were very appreciative and had many thoughts about putting more species of trout in the ponds for more production.

We fished with the normal trout gear we had purchased early in the year for stream fishing including spinners and metal lures, worms, and night crawlers. Each member and their children could keep five trout on each fishing day but had to post the catch at the gate going out of the lake area. This about the best trout fishing the club ever had. Many were interested in being on the fishing commit-tee and it became a far bigger group. More activities were scheduled to answer to the members.

Beaverkill River

Beaverkill River starts where the Willowemoc Creek ends at Junction Pool. From there, it doubles in size and flows 44.2 miles down to the Delaware River. Beaverkill River is one of the most famous fly-fishing streams in America and certainly proclaimed as such in New York State.

The fishing season is April 1st until November. Fish species include rainbow, brown, and brook trout. The best times to fish are in mornings and evenings. Fly fishing hatches include olives, caddis, blue quills, stoneflies, and March browns.

There are many access areas to the river and they are well-marked. There is a great deal of information about tackle, reels, fishing rods and lines, and many angler tips on the Beaverkill Angler website.

Summer: Fishing at Whaley Lake

During the later days of June, we continued to fish at Whaley Lake. We went trout fishing in Catskills Mountains in New York and Pennsylvania in the spring. We also joined the Whortlekill Rod and Gun Club during the same period. The club has a private lake in Hopewell Junction stocked with a lot of trout. We fished there for about two months and volunteered to be on the lake committee, but since we had no bass in the lake, we looked forward to have the bass season open. Whaley Lake was a perfect fit again. But before we went to Whaley, we decided to find a boat with a motor. That way, we could enjoy the whole lake and the two ponds beyond the railroad tracks for the bass season. The season started on the third week of June.

Mike was reading the *Southern Dutchess* newspaper and found an ad for a fourteen-foot boat with oars. The ad also listed a local telephone number. At that time, the telephone company only gave service to four party phone lines, so it took several calls. We finally talked to the owner of the boat and he agreed we could come over and see the items. The list included an Evinrude outboard motor with a 10-horsepower gasoline engine and a base stand with a test barrel. The boat was about twenty years old and was only $100. (While I was at Castle Point Veterans Hospital checking out my newly repaired hearing aid, I read in the *Southern Dutchess* that the same type of boat was listed for sale at $500!) In the 1960s, when we were looking for a boat, the owner of the boat we purchased had recently died and the wife was selling it to get rid of it, since she had no use for it. We jumped on the $100. Our boat, no doubt about it, was an excellent buy and was just what we had been looking for. We put the boat on Mike's car, while the test barrel and the two oars were in my station wagon, and we brought everything to Mike's house. The next calendar day was a Saturday, and we had the day off. We put the Evinrude engine in the test rack, filled the test barrel with water to half full, cleaned the spark plug, put some gasoline in the engine, set the choke, and pulled the starting cord. After a few pulls, lo and behold, it started right up! I shared the cost of the whole shebang with Mike, and we were anxious to take it to Whaley Lake for some bass fishing!

June 15th came about and we went that weekend to see what it was like to have a boat and engine to cross Whaley Lake. We paid the docking fee, placed all our gear in the boat, and jumped in. We had filled the gas tank on the engine with gasoline when we were at home, so we were excited to get to the other side of the lake. With the engine running, we soon discovered that we had no oars with us! This was not a good omen, as we later found out, but we decided to go anyway. After all we had a motor. We were sure the boat would take us where we wanted to go. We did not fish on the way across the lake for we had decided to see the other side of the tracks. The ponds were just encouraging us to land the boat on the bank near the largest small pond. We cut the engine and pulled the boat onto the shore. We spent some time getting used to the environment around the pond and decided to cast a few lines with our fishing gear. We tried a few popper lures but we were both disappointed. We did not get any hits even after about a half an hour of careful casting. We then decided to get back in the boat and to reconnoiter with one of the closest islands. We loaded our rods into the boat and Mike started to push the boat out into the water. I was at the helm of the motor, and as soon as we entered the water, I started the engine. We were moving slowly out toward the lake when Mike jumped into the front of the boat so as not to get wet and proceeded to fall into the bow of the boat.

Mike weighed about 299 pounds when he struck the bow considering his momentum going forward. This pushed the bow of the boat under the small wave approaching us. We hit the next wave, which neither of us saw coming. A speedboat was heading south close to the shore at a considerable speed and made a large wave approaching us. This wave engulfed our bow area. The bow now was completely in the water. The engine was still running and the wave slammed the boat even deeper into the water. The boat now became like a submarine diving and the whole boat went underwater. Both of us were sent clear but we were now swimming in the lake swimming for our lives. Fully clothed, we pedaled to stay afloat. Our gear all went under the water in about a twelve to fifteen feet. The boat was just bobbing up and down in a vertical movement. Mike, being afraid that I might drown, shoved one of our cushions to help me to stay afloat. He is a much better swimmer than I am. I grabbed the cushion and I saw my wallet floating away from me. I grabbed for it and pushed it down into my hip pocket, not knowing that the pocket was torn when the boat went down, and when I put the now folded wallet back into my pocket, it again was washed back into the deepwater and headed for the bottom. I saw it going and released the cushion and risked reaching under the water to grab the wallet but was not able to catch it as it went quickly to the bottom. Our gear of course was also all the way to the bottom. The speedboat by this time had passed us and was in the act of turning about to see if they could help us. They were dressed in swimsuits and had suitable gear for diving. They told us they would dive and recover whatever they could and were very sorry this had happened. Our gear was retrieved and our fishing poles were also found. My wallet of course was gone forever. Mike and I dragged the boat to shallower water and emptied the boat of water and everything seemed okay except for the loss of my wallet, which was still at the bottom of the lake. Unfortunately that was where all of my documents, my fishing license, my New York State driver's license, and my favorite $2 bill ended up never to be seen again. After our accident, we were still okay and all of our documents could be replaced.

We checked the gas in the engine. It seemed clear. The oil was definitely affected and we did see foamy light gray oil seeping out of the engine area. We still had no oars and our speedboat friends asked if we needed a tow. We said, "Let's see if the engine will start." Lo and behold after several pulls, the engine did start! Gray oil was still seeping out and it allowed us to move the boat under power. We said that we will take a chance on heading back to the dock. We kept the rpm low and headed to the dock. Our friends from the speedboat kept a close eye on us and shouted to us, "Good luck!" when we arrived at the dock. They gave us a hardy hand wave and motored off. We decided to take the boat and gear and headed home with no fish. We would deal with the engine later. We also thought that maybe the next day would be the better solution. We followed that maybe and had the engine running well the next day when we replaced the oil and did some cleanup. We tested the engine and used the boat for the next few outings. We were happy that we could do some more fishing with it.

Salmon
Fishing
In
Alaska

Author: **BOB SHAFER**

CHAPTER 18

Salmon Fishing in Alaska

Arrival in Alaska

I had always wanted to try salmon fishing. Little did I know that I would get multiple opportunities and at a reasonable cost.

My son-in-law was in the US Air Force and stationed at Elmendorf AFB, shared by the US Army at nearby Anchorage, Alaska, for a six-month period. Because of the length of this assignment, Tom and his wife (my daughter Trina) planned on purchasing a home off base to gain financial equity rather than renting at air force housing. Tom was able to gain compensation from the air force.

As soon as they purchased their home, they invited my wife Joyce and I to visit. As an enticement, Tom said, "I just want to say that Alaska has some of the best salmon fishing sites in the world!"

Trina suggested that summer was a great time to visit since daily temperatures in from June to August average sixty-five to seventy-five degrees Fahrenheit. That in itself was enough enticement.

Alaska beckoned and my wife and I were eager to go. The flight via Delta Airways was eleven hours and without incident. We arrived on Saturday, June 18, 1996. Tom, Trina, my grandson Mitch, and granddaughter Leah were there to welcome us upon our arrival. Saturday evening, we rested from the long trip and planned our activities for the week.

Sunday, Tom suggested, "Let's go the Base Sports Store where we can check the cost of renting waders, fishing poles, and other fishing gear."

Trina added, "We don't have to worry about waders for you, Dad. Tom and I went to a garage sale and found an insulated pair of waders which will fit you fine."

I said, "Great."

While at the Base Sports Store, we inquired about the cost of fishing licenses and purchased several Salman flies and riggings. The cost of a three-day fishing license was $35 and a seven-day license was $55. We rented a pair of waders for Tom at $3.

Later we toured downtown Anchorage and stopped in the sporting goods department of a large store. There we found excellent pricing on complete fishing pole and reel outfits. The prices were very reasonable, both purchase and rentals. We decided to purchase instead of rent.

We selected two rod and reel outfits (Tom and Trina had their own), additional streamers, and fishing boots for Trina. My credit card took a big first hit. I told Tom, "When we leave for home, we will leave all of these and you will have all new gear."

The store sold licenses at the sporting goods counter. We decided to purchase three-day licenses and scheduled the license dates for Tuesday through Thursday. Although she had some doubts, we bought a license for Joyce.

Tom said, "We have boots and poles for my son Mitch and Joyce at home." Mitch had talked about wanting to pan for gold, so I bought a couple of pans designed for panning gold in a stream. We did use the pans on an outing the next day, panning for gold on a small stream, and because of the lack of success panning in the wild, a vendor that had small amounts of gold in water buckets panned for a minimal fee.

At home that night, we had a tasty barbecued beef steak dinner with beef bought from the PX that day. I also bought a Chaps Ralph Lauren light jacket at the PX. It was a bright red and the sleeves were dark blue. I have that jacket today after wearing it for more than twenty years and I use it every spring and fall.

Typical Tourists

The first trip to Alaska in 1996 was the only trip for Joyce, as she had work requirements back in New York. We took many efforts to get her involved with fishing and entertainment available in nearby Anchorage, from watching movies at IMAX, going to restaurants, travelling to other areas in Alaska, a ship excursion to see the ice calving at the glaciers, and panning for gold.

Sunday we wanted to get some of the touristy things done. Trina found a tour boat ride in a local newspaper with a day trip for viewing glaciers. It left from a town called Whittier so off we went. Tom and Trina's van was perfect for the six of us as we traveled south on Seward Highway to Portage Glacier Road and then to Whittier tunnel. There we booked a train ride through the tunnel to the harbor. The tunnel was bored through a small mountain in 1943 by the US Army as a more direct route to Prince William Sound. During World War II, the town of Whittier was Alaska's main supply link and a major shipping port for the war effort. The tunnel proved to be indispensable. It was the only freight and passenger access, other than the sea, to the town of Whittier for fifty-five years. In the late 1990s, it was enlarged to allow alternate train and vehicular traffic. The tunnel exits at the boat docks and the docks were the boarding site for the cruise.

With time to spare, we wandered around the town. At the local museum, we learned about Whittier's history. A short time later, we boarded the cruise ship Emerald of the Sea.

The cost was roughly $100 each for the half-day tour that brought the ship within five hundred feet of the glaciers. The cruise ship held about two hundred tourists. The only offering on the ship's lunch menu was salmon. I might like fishing, but unfortunately, I dislike eating fish as a meal. Even ketchup could not hide the oily taste of the salmon as I tried to make an effort to at least try a salmon dish midway through the cruise.

The glaciers were fantastic, but they did not listen to the boat's spokesman as he said over and over again, "The glacier is about to calve any moment now!"

The captain of the ship was funny as he kept repeating, "Any minute now!" in reference to the calving of the ice. Lunch on the ship had been burgers. Little did I know that the burger was salmon and I really didn't like fish but I bravely tried it.

After a considerable time, the glacier finally did calve!

On Monday, we went to a museum in Anchorage. The displays and movie at the museum were about the Good Friday, March 27, 1964, earthquake that destroyed most of the local harbors and literally wiped out downtown Anchorage. Measuring 9.2 on the Richter scale, the earthquake was a disaster of epic proportions and was the strongest earthquake that had ever happened in this time period. The tsunami devastated Seward and other bay areas. The damage was well documented and nearly unbelievable.

Fishing in the Russian River

Tom said, "I will ask my air force buddies at the air base about salmon fishing including where and when it would be best to go on fishing for salmon." Tom's friends were quite knowledgeable about the area's fisheries. They had personal experience and information that would certainly help. This certainly helped and made it more doable and affordable. They helped with license fees and where to purchase them. They were familiar with the restrictions, the best fishing rivers, timing of the salmon runs, access to the most popular fishing spots, and entertainment. The US Army furnished lodging for two days and nights at the army facility. The lodge helped in setting up fishing trips with minimal costs at their nearby facilities.

Our friends could help on returning runs from the sea. There are two species of salmon that have overlapping months of May through July and Chinook (king) salmon run in Ship Creek in May until the end of July, which is only a week or so apart. Sockeye (red) salmon runs peak at nearby Kenai and Russian rivers. That would also be the same as the Ship Creek's king salmon runs. As these spawning runs occur for several weeks, the right planning would put both runs right on target with our availability. What could "wet your whistle" is that even though you can only catch one king on your license, they can weigh between twenty-five to ninety pounds. The record is over a hundred pounds. Ship Creek is one of the most popular streams for king fishing and it runs from the dam at the fishing hatchery, north, through the city of Anchorage to the sea. The average weights for kings caught there is twenty-five and fifty pounds and are around thirty to forty inches in length. Two hours from Anchorage would put you at the Kenai and Russian rivers, two of the most famous salmon rivers in Alaska. There, the Sockeye would grow to about twenty inches in length with an average weight of eight to nine pounds.

At this time, you can switch to sockeyes but it is not legal to fish for kings on the Russian River until later in July. But your reward when fishing on the Kenai could be a forty- to fifty-pound sockeye salmon (Reds) on any given day of those runs. The next year, in 1997, on my second trip to Alaska, I went a little later in the month of July to be able to match the king salmon runs. We went to the Kenai and met a new Russian friend. He and his wife worked at the local cannery, and we talked about fishing for salmon and he told me about his work at the cannery and persuaded me to let him clean my take. He was really good at it too. It couldn't be nicer and we met several times in the next couple of years.

Trina called and made a reservation for us at the Forest Service Campground at Mile 52 on the Sterling Highway. The Russian River flows from the Upper Russian River Lake, then through another lake, and joins the Kenai River three miles down the highway. The stream has a fly-only, single hookup restriction.

The use of fly for bait is a misnomer as most salmon do not feed once they have left saltwater and arrive in the freshwaters. The clear water of the Russian allows you to see the fish passing by. The method used is called lined (snagged in the mouth). If a salmon is snagged anywhere else but the mouth or gill area of the fish, it must be released. Anglers have the choice of fishing with fly rods or spinning rods.

The fly-only designation is for the terminal end of your line. This allows outfits with appropriate weights.

Fish in the Russian River can be expected to average twenty inches in length and weigh up to ten pounds. We had a thirty-pound test monofilament line and we thought that weight line would be adequate. We did notice that most anglers used a heavier line and we soon found out why! The Russian River is definitely combat-style fishing, which is the most noticeable at the confluence of the Kenai River. That area of the Russian River is called the sanctuary and is where the salmon rest between runs. It is opened for fishing when authorities are sure that there are adequate fish in the spawning run to meet replacement goals.

The Russian River is lined with board walkways to minimize erosion and fish stations available to clean any salmon caught. When we arrived at the campground, we ate lunch and got ready to fish. We set up our poles and donned our boots, fishing vests, and waders. We followed the walkways to the stream where we all wet our lines for the first time.

We entered the stream. There was plenty of evidence that salmon had been caught here, and at the stations, it was obvious that the run had passed through the area. The only fish we saw there were some scared trout.

Joyce was having trouble with her gear. I patiently tried to show her how to cast. It was to no avail. She was not a fisher-person and she ultimately gave up. She sat on the bank of the stream and read a book she had brought just in case. Enjoying the outdoors, she never noticed the length of the day. The sun just seemed to hang in there. In Alaska this time of the year, you can get daylight just about twenty-four hours in a day. The summer solstice was arriving.

Joining Anglers on the Kenai

Realizing that the salmon weren't there, Tom, Mitch, and I decided to walk the boardwalks downstream and check out the sanctuary. When we got there, fishing was in full combat mode. We were near the edge of the Kenai River on a fast-running section of the stream. We mixed in with the anglers on the bank of the upper sanctuary. There definitely was fish there and the anglers were shouting the proverbial, "Fish on!" If they could do it, so could we! Maneuvering into tight openings, as best we could, we cast into the water with what we thought was an appropriate manner, but neither of us was catching anything.

As I watched the other anglers, I could see how they used a drift method in fast water, flipping their wrists to hook any salmon that inadvertently swam into their line, resulting in quite a few successful catches. I could not help but notice that we were being outfished by two ladies, who were fishing with fly rods using heavy lines and filled their limit while we watched. Obviously they knew secrets we did not know.

We had been fishing with no success, consistently losing the fish. This finally struck me as being my fault for not realizing our mistake—we tied a knot in our lines and this had been so successful in catching small trout back home. Sometimes the line just untied from the hook and sinker arrangement when the salmon took advantage of the fast water and lunged downstream. It was difficult to hold the fish with such light line. I asked one fisherman who seemed to have a special line that looked like wire and he said that it was a hundred pounds. Our line was only thirty pounds with an attached fly and sinker hookups that were only twenty pounds. We needed to purchase heavy line like the other fishermen and tie that directly to the fly. We temporarily utilized the thirty-pound line but still had trouble playing out the fish because of the fast water and the nearness of the other fishermen. The next time I am going fishing at Ship Creek or the Kenai for kings, I will certainly make sure we have heavier line.

We had fished from the time we arrived and had walked several miles. It was late so we decided that we were done for the day. We hadn't paid that much attention to the time. The summer solstice was upon us. It was 11:30 p.m. and we still had sunshine. As we left the Kenai River, we noticed that other fishermen were just coming out to fish. Our time at the campsite had expired so we began heading back to Anchorage. It was strange to go through the entire day and not see the nightfall. Driving back, we did not even turn on our headlights. Businesses were open 24/7 and advertised the solstice on their billboards for the next week.

Fishing in Anchorage at Ship Creek

The next trip would be in 1997. I flew alone via American Airways since Joyce would be home and working at Montgomery Ward in Poughkeepsie. I had plenty of vacation time and wanted to fly to Alaska for a seven- to eight-day (second) trip to Anchorage. Joyce was very good about my fishing and hunting activities. I left around July that year to be able to catch the king salmon runs at the Kenai River and Ship Creek.

Ship Creek is unique to salmon fishing because of the creek's locale, but mostly because it's a hatchery supported river. Elmendorf Hatchery controls the stream above the dam. It is just beyond the legal fishing area located on the north bank of the Ship Creek, near the intersection of Reeve Boulevard and Post Road. It needs about five hundred king salmon to support the continued existence of the fishery. King salmon fishing runs from May to July during the fishing season. When we were there, a contestant won $100 with a forty-pound king.

Coho salmon runs are just after the king salmon runs. They are popular from July to August. Specially tagged fish prizes were available from $100 to $10,000 on all contests held by the local merchants. The fishermen who entered the contests were very happy and contributed to appropriate ticket sales.

The king salmon runs have approximately 4,700 fish. The creek also supports small runs of humpback salmon (pink). On even years, it supports sockeye salmon (silver) and after the king salmon runs (yearly) during the fall. These two runs occur separately.

Highway and Street Side Access

There are very few highways in Alaska. Alaska has the least number of highways in the United States. The Alaskan Highway is actually located in Canada and is the leading highway to get to Alaska itself. This highway is used mostly for commercial operations mainly in mountain terrain. It is very crowded and dangerous during most of ice and snow periods. Once you get to the Canadian and

Alaskan border, there are only three highways that you can choose to get near to the city of Anchorage—Seward Highway from the south, Parks Highway from the north, and Glenn Highway from the west. All these converge in the city of Anchorage. No doubt about it, it is better to fly into Elmendorf Airport and rent a car.

Ship Creek is located in urban Anchorage on the north side of the city. It can be difficult to locate. Ship Creek can be fished on both sides of the creek. To access both sides of the creek, you can walk across the dam or drive to one of the parking lot pay stations. Many locals do this. The south bank can be accessed by traveling on E Avenue to North C Street and taking a right on North Street and a right turn onto Ship Creek Avenue. The north bank can be accessed from North C Street and turning right on Whitney Road. The fees for the parking areas are very small. The fishing area that is accessible on foot is only about a half to three quarters of a mile long. A steel cable is stretched across the stream and designates the upstream legal fishing limit. This is the only place from there down to the Knick Ann of Cook's outlet.

Be sure that you follow the guidelines in booklets available from vendors about the tide timings both for mornings and through-out the day. The entire length from this point is tidal controlled. Sometimes you will see a fishing boat in the tidal waters possibly as deep as twenty feet; hopefully if it's your boat, be sure it is capable of doing this. It is important to realize the depth the tide can attain. The tide, even at the start of the area near the cable, can be up to your chin or even deeper in the channel area. When the tide is com-ing in, make sure that you don't accidently drown! If necessary, get back to shore immediately. You can still fish from the rocky areas and roadside accesses. The inner banks are lined with mud from the bay inlet to just below the dam. Only the channel of the stream is gravel. One side of the river is rock lined and can be accessed for about five hundred feet without mud and this site gets very crowded.

A local motel backs right up to this point in the stream and it is very popular at this site. Staying there can be costly, but what the heck!

If you are adventurous wearing waders, you can access the channel in the middle of the creek during the slack periods of the tide. It is very popular because most of the king salmon are caught in this channel, but if you fish the channel, you must fish within site of the dam. The suction of the mud on the shores downstream or near the channel is near forgiving. If you get stuck in it as the tide is rising, you might have to be airlifted out, especially near the mouth of the inlet. The high tide at the inlet can be twenty feet, and from there, it reaches the dam at four to six feet in depth. The creek water at tide change goes both ways at considerable speed. A word to the wise should be sufficient. At low tide, a really ambitious and nervy fisherman using waders and a staff pole can actually cross the creek to both parking areas near the cable.

Our Last Days Spent as Tourists

Panning for gold (unsuccessfully) at one of the state forests preserves and a sightseeing to Seward visiting shops and the locale completed our daily trips.

The scenery is really gorgeous along the highway. Some of the mountaintops still had snow and were magnificent. All the mountain ranges in that area are above the tree line. We saw Dall sheep that ventured down from the top of the mountains to the roadside. They were really beautiful.

We stopped at a restaurant complete with an Alaskan theme, stuffed bears and all, and had a really great meal. We purchased a few knickknacks and an Alaska hat for me. The next day, we left for home and promised to return.

I could not resist and promised additional trips and ended up coming back four more times.

Return to Ship Creek

The second year at Ship Creek had the makings of a disaster. As I became more knowledgeable about fishing there, I also became more daring when it came to fish the channel areas during the slack tide periods. As I fished the channel, with the tide lowering near slack level, I hooked into a nice fish that gave me a pretty good battle! The line kept going out and I wanted to catch this fish. I managed to get my catch closer to my side of the channel, not an easy task, because of all the fishermen present. I did not have my net available, but one of the fishermen asked if I wanted his help. I accepted and turned to coach the fish to where it could be netted. It was a king salmon weighing about thirty pounds.

Suddenly, as I turned to get closer to the fish, the riverbank collapsed under me and I found myself swimming in the creek! The water was cold and deep. As I floated, I realized that I was in immediate danger! Luckily, I had tied the waders tightly. I was actually being held by the fish I had hooked and swung toward the channel's edge. I didn't panic but found it difficult to get back to the edge. Holding the rod high, I managed to get a toehold and was able to stand and gain purchase on the ridge of the channel again.

When I finally got upright, everyone within sight was clapping and glad that I was out of danger. My friend asked if I wanted to keep this fish. Together, my fellow fisherman and I netted the fish and asked if I was going to keep the salmon. I had considered it before the swimming effort, but when I thought it out, I said, "Yes!" He proceeded to push a small spiked instrument into the top of the king's head and it stopped flopping around. My king was about thirty pounds in weight and nearly forty inches in length. I had a hard time holding him above the water. I was through fishing for the day at that point, and I had the one king allowed by law. I thanked my friend and started back to shore. During the fish fight, the tide had increased and I barely got back to shore by changing directions to keep me from getting wet. I brought the fish back to Trina and Tom's house and cleaned it in the small stream there and placed it into their freezer.

Fishing on the Talkeetna

The following year, we made changes to our activities. We branched out to different streams and ocean fishing. Being active military, Tom was able to get reservations at an army recreational center in Seward, Alaska. We stayed in a large motel-like building that had all the amenities you might need. We used that for two occasions.

The first occasion was a jet boat half-day excursion ride for salmon fishing on the Talkeetna River. These are twenty-four- to twenty-seven-foot boats custom-built with inboard engines and a water-jet exhaust that propelled the boats to speeds of up to 35 mph. They were capable of operating in as little as eight inches of water. This outing was scheduled by the army facility for four hours of fishing.

The both streams were too deep for me to cross. Several boats came up to and passed our fishing area. Unfortunately the salmon that might have been in that river must have moved on. The boat captain dropped us off in a parklike area after a one-hour trip upriver. We left the lodge at 7:30 a.m. and the boat would be back to pick us up at 12:30 p.m. We were awestruck with the beauty and remoteness of the surroundings. The scenery was beautiful to behold. We were at the confluence of another stream and it had several deep pool areas. The Talkeetna River was approximately a hundred feet wide with fast-flowing glacially cold and discolored water. The intersecting stream was clear and it made a barrier that we felt sure was where the salmon would swim along on their trip upriver. The salmon must have been on vacation.

We intended to catch any salmon combination that should have been running in the river, but we were unsuccessful in catching them. We did attempt to catch trout that were breaking water in several breakwater areas but to no avail. Disappointed with no salmon, we slapped a lot of water. We returned to the recreational center with little excitement but for the beauty of the river valley and looked into more fishing activities that were available. We were able to get a power boat excursion through the recreational facility from Seward into ocean waters fishing for halibut and sea bass.

Deep-Sea Fishing

Tom and Trina were able to arrange a charter from the recreational facility and bought my ticket as a birthday gift there. They chartered the boat so we could fish for Halibut. This area was quite quiet but access to the sea had very high seas. The boat appeared to be hand-built and was solid-looking but not handsome. We intended only to fish for halibut, which were known to be as large as a hundred pounds, but the sea ended up to be too much and later on came to safer waters and fished for sea bass. The boat climbed the waves and when it crested fell back with smashing blows. I always get seasick under power and this ended up as no exception. I was doing fine until most of the fishermen got ill and passed the bucket. When it got to me, unfortunately, I contributed with the others as the smell from the bucket overtook whatever stomach power I had. I passed it on after making my donation.

The captain started to worry about the size of the waves and he radioed the coast guard and other boats. We were not able to stay in the areas ideal for halibut fishing. To salvage the trip, we headed closer to shore where the water was more stable.

On the way, we spotted the beautiful sight, two whales blowing, just ahead of us! When we reached the calmer waters, we started fishing. The captain handed me a rod that was weighted with very large metal weights. It was difficult to use and but it allowed the weight to sink near the bottom, where the black bass were. I was still ill from the seasickness but I continued to fish. The captain gave me credit for fishing while most of the others were too sick to manage. Pointing to one of the fishermen lying prone on a bunk, he said, "I don't know why that kid over there ever goes out fishing. This is about his fifth trip with me and he never gets to fish."

Tom and I caught fifteen sea bass between us. They were about three to five pounds each and were extremely hard to boat. I did not like fishing with such heavy weights necessary to get the bait to the bottom. It was difficult to get the weight near to the bottom or even upward to check my bait without a struggle.

At least the trip was successful in that we had caught something. We did see boats bring in halibut weighing around a hundred pounds, but it was not for us to get such a prize!

Returning to the Russian River Sanctuary

We did get to do some more salmon fishing at the confluence of the Russian River with the Kenai. We were there to catch sockeye salmon that were approximately ten pounds each and about fifteen inches in length. We stopped at the Sportsman's Landing at Milepost 55 of the Seward Highway and paid a small fee of $2.50. We took the ferry over the Kenai to the opposite shore where we spent the day having a really good time at the Russian River Sanctuary.

We had learned that the reds run quite close to the shore as opposed to the kings that stay in the deeper fast-flowing water. Fishing the edge of the discolored water from the Kenai and the clear water from the Russian was very productive.

I looked down into the water where I spotted a flash. I thought it was a fish but it was too small. I reached into the water and retrieved a cell phone, which was obviously lost by some fisherman. We took it home intending to return it to the owner if we could only get it operational. I never did find out what happened to that phone.

Mitch had trouble filling his limit. A local who worked at the cannery was really good at catching fish and he offered to help Mitch. He was a nice guy but we had to say no after the second fish. After all, reeling in someone else's catch is not very thrilling. We left satisfied that we had caught our share.

Fishing on the Russian for the Last Time

On my next trip, Tom was on temporary duty (TDY) in Korea. With Tom on the phone and Trina and I at the local Ford dealer, I helped them negotiate the purchase of a 1998 Ford Expedition. Mitch and I used the Expedition on our next fishing trips.

The next time I would see Tom was at a family outing in Las Vegas after he had retired from the US Air Force.

Mitch and I were on our own. We made two trips. One was a third trip to the Russian River where both Mitch and I filled our limits. We were at the campsite's fish cleaning station and I was attempting, with limited success, to clean the salmon. Our friend of last year from the cannery came by and recognized me. He offered to clean the fish. He was very skillful and within fifteen minutes had cleaned all twelve of the salmon we had caught.

Fishing on the Kenai for Salmon

We wanted to try another area for kings. On the next road trip, we stopped at a different campsite that bordered on the Kenai and the confluence of the Cooper River. We fished there for a couple of hours without any luck. I moved upstream to the spot where the Cooper River met the Kenai and started fishing there. No one was catching any salmon at that point. We were in between active runs. I spotted a log on the opposite bank. I switched poles to a nine-foot fly rod that I had purchased in the department store where we had bought our original outfits. The rod's action had a substantially stiff feel. Using that action and whipping the rod back and forth, I flipped the salmon rig toward the log. I made believe that I was trout fishing and let the lure float toward and eventually under the log. When the lure got there, I felt a tug on the line and knew right away that a salmon had struck my lure and the fight was on.

This was different and somewhat unexpected because most salmon when they arrive in freshwater do not feed during the spawning run. The fish gave me a decent fight and I knew I could land him. When I was asked if I wanted help in landing the fish, I respectfully declined. I was able to land the fish without a net by grabbing the fish by the gills. Although not large, it weighed in at twenty-four pounds. It proved to be the last fish that I would catch in Alaska.

Trina and Tom were planning to move to Idaho for Tom's next air force assignment and this would be my last trip. Trina asked me to take as much fish with me as I could because their freezer was full from all the fishing we had done in the last two years and they had to put the freezer into storage. I purchased a shipping container and filled it to the brim. All our friends had salmon.

American Airways was very helpful on my last trip. They accepted the packaging of the salmon and bent the rules to allow the quote "dry ice." They said, "You did say ice, didn't you?" Oops, did I say that?

A FICTIONAL SHORT STORY

Assassination of Presidential Candidates

"President Tush of the United States has been meeting with Homeland Security, Secret Service, and FBI officials for several hours now. It has been established that the terrorists were homegrown Americans intending on doing as much damage as they could to American will and esteem. No, Middle East has yet to announce their support. We suspect that there will be multiple responses," Ben Shook, CPT News correspondent, reporting.

Nancy Whosit said, "Ben, take it from here! We've gotten 7 Middle Eastern countries responding. North Korea, Iran, Serbia, Yemen, Sudan, Somalia, and Libya have all put on a sideshow. All seven countries have declared a consortium and intend to start a full-scale terrorist attacks on the United States, Canada, Granada, Britain,

France, Japan, and Israel. Iran, Serbia, and North Korea have all said they would consider using nukes and chemical attacks. Russia and China have not reported support of any of the involved countries. This has the potential of becoming a full-scale world war. Breaking news just in. Clayton and Ipana are both dead!"

"Ben Shook, CPT News correspondent, reporting. Coordinated attacks by bomb-laden terrorists killed both leading democratic candidates at their respective campaign headquarters just moments ago. We are reporting from outside democratic headquarters here in Washington. We will bring you pictures from within headquarters as soon as the equipment can be brought online. Bill Small, our veteran election correspondent, is inside coordinating efforts. Bill, how is it going in there?"

"Ben, the scene is incredible. The Secret Service is now trying to get a handle on the disaster and is asking our cooperation not to go into the explosion areas as of this time. Back to you, Ben!"

"In unbelievably accurate attacks, bomb-laden terrorists posing as loyal supporters approached both Clayton and Ipana detonating bombs that instantly killed both candidates and two secret service agents. Eighteen staff members, supporters, and several Secret Service agents were severely injured. All the wounded are being brought to local hospitals. Six of the injured have been judged as critical.

"Using foreign terrorist techniques common in the Middle East, both terrorists were wearing explosive vests packed with enough high explosive and ball bearings to shatter the podium areas along with the victims and the attacking terrorists. As of this moment, a total of six, including the bombers, are dead and the total number of casualties is expected to rise. CPT newsmen and cameras not damaged in the explosions are now being brought back online. The picture you are seeing now is the Democratic Washington headquarters. Heavy smoke is hiding the extensive damage caused by the explosions. Two terrorists detonated bombs with near-simultaneous precision within several feet of the candidates. The explosions instantly killed both of the leading democratic contenders, Secret Service personnel, and others as the candidates were addressing supporters in preparation for the debate scheduled for two o'clock this afternoon.

"Speculation is running rampant. No one has yet has claimed responsibility for this attack, nor has any evidence surfaced as to any individual or organization that may have been behind it. Everyone even remotely connected to the campaigns is suspect. The impact of this attack is staggering. Democrats and Republicans are in a state of shock and you can expect comments from both parties shortly on CPT News. Heavy reinforcements from the Secret Service augmented by the FBI are pouring into the area and can be seen combing the scene for evidence. I have just been informed that President Tush has just been informed and is about to comment. CPT will cover the president's speech as soon as he arrives at the White House press headquarters. Nancy Whosit is in the press room at this time. Nancy, just when do you expect the president?"

"Thanks, Ben. Nancy Whosit, CPT News. President Tush is expected to arrive at the newsroom in about five minutes. He is now meeting with Homeland Security, Secret Service, and FBI officials to gather the latest information available before addressing the nation. Here he is now."

"My fellow Americans, the assassinations of two of our leading Democratic politicians, senators Clayton and Ipana, will no doubt be remembered as the worst political disaster in history. It is with the greatest sorrow that I address the nation now in this moment of sadness. The interruption of the political system with the deaths of both of the Democratic Party's leading candidates is unequivocally one of the most dastardly acts ever conceived. Let me assure you that no effort will be spared to find the guilty party or parties involved. At this time, I am directing all security agencies to place immediate priority in finding the source of this horrendous act. No effort is to be spared. I will address the nation later this evening when we can further address this calamity. Thank you and God bless America."

"President Tush has just completed a brief address to the nation. Democratic leaders have just announced that the party will continue the party efforts to field a viable candidate for president. Further information will be forthcoming in an official announcement scheduled for six o'clock this evening. Back to you, Ben."

"Thank you, Nancy. CPT television at this time would like to take this moment to add our sorrow and feelings of loss because of the assassinations. We will be displaying the American flag and observing a moment of silence. Following that, we will continue to cover events as they occur. Fellow Americans, we present that moment. We ask all Americans to join us in our silence. Ben Shook, CPT news correspondent."

ABOUT THE AUTHOR

From the age of three, the author grew up on the farm in Adams, Massachusetts, and loved every bit of the shared experiences with his family and new friends. School and farm activities were the builders of his potential.

The next four years of his life was filled with new activities. New jobs, fishing, hunting, and hiking to the top of Mount Greylock built his character and strength.

He served for four years in the US Air Force and then had job experiences at GE and IBM leading to huge strides in personal growth. Later, other jobs kept his life interesting.

This is a solid proof about growing up in United States.

CPSIA information can be obtained
at www.ICGtesting.com
Printed in the USA
BVHW092024080320
574407BV00004B/24